NOTED!

Kathy J. Jacobson

To Jerry –

with blessings!

Kathy J. Jacobson

LITTLE CREEK PRESS®
A DIVISION OF KRISTIN MITCHELL DESIGN, INC.

Mineral Point, Wisconsin USA

Dedication

For Daniel

Acknowledgements

I am grateful to those who gave me insights into their worlds, experiences, and knowledge, especially Carly Edwards, RN; Emily Hanson, DPT; and Judy Ramacitti, RN; Ellen Snoeyenbos, librarian; and Nahldean Knebel. Also, I thank the nurses and CNAs with whom I work in hospice, who constantly inspire me with their dedication to the sick and dying.

A special thank you to friend, Terri Ellis, and daughter, Kirsten Jacobson, for reading the manuscript and making important suggestions. Much gratitude to my family, husband, Jeff Jacobson, daughter, Kirsten Jacobson, and sons, Spencer Jacobson and Jens Jacobson for their love and support throughout the years.

I also truly appreciate the work of my editor, Diane Franklin, and thank publisher, Kristin Mitchell, for giving me this opportunity.

Chapter One

"I got the job!" Jillian announced to her daughter, Marty, as they chatted over their laptop screens. Jillian was sprawled across the floral print bedspread in the stale hotel room like a teenager. She had been living like this for a week while looking for work in the Los Angeles area. She smoothed a wrinkle beneath her and tried not to think about how many germs were on the suspect bedcover, her concern stemming from many years working in the nursing field. She shook off the thought and returned her attention to Marty.

"Great, Mom!" Marty exclaimed, her smile lighting up the dreary surroundings. Marty, more than one person had observed, could brighten a dark room just by entering it. She almost always wore a smile and was one of the most compassionate, pleasant, and optimistic people Jillian had ever known. She was one of those people whom other people always wanted to be around. That was why Jillian made certain to video-chat every week, provided the technology was working where Marty was currently living. Her daughter's work assignment had taken her overseas, and the weeks when the technology wasn't working were long ones for Jillian. She was thrilled that it was working on this particular evening when she wanted to share her news.

"I'll be happy if it turns out to be *good*," Jillian said. "It sounds like the owner of the home goes through household help like magnesium citrate goes through...well, you know!"

"Oh, Mama, you're such a nurse," Marty replied chuckling. Marty herself was a medical intern. She was a student in Harvard Medical School's Department of Global Health and Social Medicine. She was currently on a rotation working with the World Health Organization in Senegal, researching and teaching about the prevention and treatment of the deadly disease Ebola. Marty had wanted to work in this area of medicine ever since she was ten years old. That's when she announced to her mother that when she grew up she was going to cure "river blindness" and other diseases in Africa.

"Occupational hazard, I guess," Jillian said with a slight sigh, the kind only someone intimately acquainted with the other could detect.

"What's really bothering you, Mom?" Marty asked. She could always read her mother like a book.

"You mean beside the facts that I left a great job, sold everything but the kitchen sink, and I am sitting in a rather depressing hotel room two thousand miles away from home, with two suitcases holding everything I own?"

"Mom, it's not like it's the first time you have done that," Marty reminded her.

Marty was right, of course. It was when Marty was five. Jillian was a nurse at a hospital not far from her hometown in Wisconsin. One year earlier, Jillian's dad had succumbed to cancer, and her mom, whose own health was fragile, planned to move to Florida to live with her sister and escape the cold winters of the Midwest. It seemed to Jillian like it was a good time to make a change of her own. Now that her dad was gone and her mom was moving, there was nothing, and no one, to hold her back.

While Jillian had enjoyed her work back then, she always felt a bit awkward as the only single mom in her unit. Jillian didn't have a lot of friends at that point in her life, and those she did have were more like friendly acquaintances. She didn't really fit in with the other single nurses, and neither was she a wife or a married mother. She just couldn't seem to find her niche.

The only place she had felt at ease and truly accepted was at church. Everyone was so kind and friendly, and there were several women in the women's group who took her under their wings. Some of them even watched Marty for her, becoming like surrogate grandmothers and aunts to Marty and her, especially after her parents were no longer around.

As much as she had loved her church family, Jillian had grown restless and felt that it was time to strike out on her own. She had begun a job search, but she would have never guessed where she would end up. It all began one Sunday morning when a medical missionary came to speak at their adult forum after the church service. After the presentation that day, Jillian began to investigate mission opportunities for nurses. One thing led to another, and after numerous interviews, a lot of soul-searching, and prayer, Jillian packed their bags, sold the rest of their possessions, and took an assignment as a nurse in Tanzania, East Africa. She and Marty spent the next eight years with the gracious and faithful people of that country, and they both still had many special friends there with whom they remained in contact.

Jillian sighed again, this time more heavily, and continued the conversation with Marty, twirling her long, thick hair with her fingers. "It's just that I thought I retired from nursing care," Jillian said. She recounted to her daughter the words of her new boss, Jerry Mack, the agency administrator of Happy Home Housekeeping, when he filled her in on her new position. According to Mr. Mack, the owner of the home had a painkiller addiction, stemming from a sports injury from many years ago. He was currently in recovery to his knowledge, but said that people close to the gentleman, of which there were very few, were becoming suspicious and concerned, including himself.

It didn't help that the man refused to go to the doctor, had stopped working, and wouldn't accept calls or visits from anyone, even his nephew, his closest family member. Mr. Mack had said the man, a Mr. Romano, had always been a bit on the difficult side, but he had recently reached new heights—or lows might be a better word.

"Well, Mom," Marty said, "you might be retired from nursing, but you will never be retired from caring, and you know it."

Jillian smiled slightly. She was so proud of her beautiful daughter, the best "surprise" of her life. She couldn't get away with anything with Marty and loved how they could so honestly converse, challenging one another when they needed challenging and lifting up one another when that was the best medicine.

"How did you get so smart?" she asked Marty.

Marty flashed another brilliant smile. "I had a good teacher." The computer screen froze with Marty's face still in that warming smile, then it faded to black.

Jillian gently closed the laptop, knowing there would be no more talking that night. She smiled to herself at the thought of her daughter, wondering what she had ever done to deserve being the mother of that wonderful girl.

Her mind drifted back in time to the day when she was twenty-two and heard the words that would forever change her life. "You're pregnant."

Her parents had always told her to make good decisions. They said that everyone makes some they wish they could have back, but it was best, as a rule, not to enter into situations that had life-altering consequences without great consideration and lots of prayer.

She had gone and done, without consideration or prayer, just what they had suggested she not. She had made a life-altering decision based completely on feelings of the heart—and as she was quick to find out, only *her* heart.

She traced back even further in her mind to when it all really began. It was during her sophomore year of college at the University of Wisconsin. Every Thursday night at nine p.m., she and her friends made certain they were in the lounge of their dorm floor to watch the next episode of the new, groundbreaking medical drama, *O.R.* Unless you were one of the unfortunate ones who were assigned a lab that evening, you didn't miss it for anything. So while other students on campus flooded to establishments on State Street to begin the weekend, if you were a female, and especially a female nursing student, you hustled back from the library at 8:45 p.m. to get a good spot on a couch or chair to watch the show.

She and her friends were enthralled. For the first time, a show dared to dabble in the more realistic ins and outs of the medical profession. It entered into the lives of the patients, hospital administrators, doctors, and nurses as no one had before. Then there were the operations themselves. The operating room scenes were sometimes so graphic that people had to leave the room. More than one nursing student made a decision to change majors after watching this show. Jillian, too, made a decision after watching this show. She decided that after she graduated she would go to medical school. She would finish her nursing degree, just in case things didn't work out, but she wanted to be like—correction, she wanted to *be*—the beautiful cardiac surgeon on the show, Dr. Pamela Prine, played by the actress and former Olympic swimming champion Monica Morgan. On the show, Dr. Prine was secretly involved in a romance with the Chief of Surgery, Dr. Nick Caruso, played by actor John D. Romano. Apparently they were a not-so-secret couple in real life, at least according to *TV Guide* and *People* magazine.

Dr. Nick Caruso was older than Dr. Prine, in the show and in real life, and was portrayed as serious and stoic. More than one fan of the show wondered what the writers were thinking when they made them a couple. But Jillian, like Dr. Prine/Monica Morgan, found him attractive. Her friends teased her about liking him. They said he was boring. They said he was way too old. He even limped, for goodness sake. In real life, she had heard that the limp was from a football injury. In the show, they had written the limp into the storyline as the result of a war injury sustained in Vietnam. Jillian's friends instead went crazy over all the cute medical interns on the show, who were, of course, always involved with the nurses.

When Jillian graduated, she did indeed go to medical school. She passed her nursing boards with flying colors, did a summer internship, and then headed out east. There she met and fell in love with a doctor/professor in her very first class. He was so handsome. He was so brilliant. She found him attractive, and she thought he felt the same way when midway through the semester he had asked her to stay after class. They began seeing each other soon afterward, and one thing led to another. She was certain it was true love and that when she told him about the baby he would want to marry her.

She couldn't have been more wrong. He even suggested that the child was not his. She had never been with anyone else in her life, so that was definitely not a possibility. She decided that she could not continue the program and went back home, a humbled soul. She took a position at a hospital as a nurse after all, so grateful that she had at least made one right decision in finishing her nursing degree and passing the boards.

On August 13, Marty Jo Johnson came into the world, and to this day Jillian knew that this was her greatest accomplishment in her forty-some years of life. Her daughter may have been a surprise, but she was a *good* surprise. Jillian named her child after her own adoptive father, Martin Johnson, the most wonderful man she had ever known, still to that very day. He was kind, faithful in every sense of the word, gentle yet strong, and had more integrity in his little finger than most people had in their entire bodies and souls.

Jillian had decided the minute she knew she was pregnant that Marty would be Marty one way or the other, boy or girl. Her father would have a namesake. Marty's middle name, "Jo," was Jillian's middle name, as well. Her adoptive mom, Judy, always liked the name Jill for a first name, but wanted her middle name to be "Jo," after her favorite character in her favorite book, *Little Women*. "Jill Jo" didn't sound right, so her mom had discovered the name Jillian. So Jillian Jo Johnson, it was.

After Marty was born, Jillian continued working as a nurse and earned her master's degree. Her parents were a wonderful help with Marty and were thrilled to have a grandchild. Most of their friends had many grandchildren; some of them even had great-grandchildren. But Martin and Judy had remained childless until their early forties when they adopted Jillian. So even though they may have wished Marty had come into the world under different circumstances, they were very supportive and welcomed Marty into the family with the same love they had given Jillian. They always stayed true to their mantra—"every child is a gift from God."

When Marty was three-and-a-half, her Grandpa Martin started getting sick. They thought it was nothing to be alarmed about at first, but when a cold never seemed to get better, Jillian finally convinced her father to agree to a checkup. The man had never been sick a day in his life. He was a farmer and machinist, and was always active. He didn't smoke, wasn't overweight, and had a positive outlook on life. So it was hard to swallow when the diagnosis was made—lung cancer. Jillian still wondered if it wasn't due to some of the fertilizers or other chemicals farmers sometimes come into contact with, but it didn't really matter. Cancer is cancer, no matter what started the process.

A year-and-a-half later, he was gone. Her mother had seemed to age about ten years in that time, and Jillian was concerned with her mom's decline in health. When Judy's older sister, Jillian's Aunt Sally in Florida, suggested Judy come down and move in with her, she went. She was never really the same after Martin died. Even Jillian and Marty could not seem to lift her spirits. In some ways, Jillian felt like she lost both her parents at once, even though her mom went on to live another fifteen years.

It was soon after Judy's move to Florida that Jillian and Marty went off on their "African adventure," as they sometimes referred to it in retrospect. It was one of Jillian's better decisions in life. If this current new adventure turned out half as well, she would be thrilled.

Jillian got up off the bed and gazed around the room. There was a cheap painting of a sailboat moored on a sandy beach on the wall, the frame tilted to one side. She tried to straighten it a couple of times, but it kept sliding back to the same position, so she finally gave up. This would be her final night in the hotel, thank goodness. Perhaps she should have gone for something nicer, but she hadn't been sure how long it would take her to find employment, especially the kind she had in mind.

She had been looking for a position that would not be mentally taxing, wanting to save her brain for her writing, as she put it. She also wanted something "live-in" to keep her costs down. She had saved decently over the past ten years, but wanted to use that money to publish her book—well, the book she was *hoping* to write after she got settled in.

She planned to use her personal and professional experiences as the basis of her writing. She had gone to a writing seminar, and the leaders had explained how writers often began their books with a blog, which could later lead to a book with the same theme.

The blog posts and comments would give her material for the book and might even help her build a fan base.

Jillian had decided to call her blog "Where Broken Hearts Go," and she hoped to help others who were struggling with hurts of the heart. She wanted to give them hope and encouragement, as well as tips on how to deal with painful situations in healthy, productive, and faithful ways. She had seen too many people turn to self-destructive behaviors to deal with their hurts, which made their situations even worse. She wanted to help others avoid these. Jillian also knew how valuable it was to have someone to talk to, to share one's pain with, even if it was only a place to "go" online.

Jillian felt like an expert in the broken heart area. She never seemed to fall in love with the right person. In high school, she was asked out by a decent number of boys, but never by those she liked. Instead, it was always the ones who didn't ask her out who caught her interest.

In college, she dated the same young man for two years. He was very kind and hard-working. She met him through a girl on her dorm floor whose job it was to find a date for her boyfriend's buddy, Dave, from Babcock House, the agricultural fraternity. It was the fraternity's annual Winter Formal, and Jillian was the lucky one free for the occasion.

Dave was a nice guy who planned to be a dairy farmer. He was always thoughtful and respectful, and Jillian liked him, but she had not been in love with him. She had also known that his deep roots would never allow him to leave the state, let alone the family farm. She broke off the relationship midway through their senior year, using the excuse that the rigors of medical school would not allow for a relationship, especially one that was long-distance. During some of the rougher times of her life, she reflected that perhaps she should have just married Dave and settled down on the farm, which could have been a good life. But then she remembered that if she had done that, there would be no Marty, and that would have been the greatest heartbreak of all.

Jillian put the few articles of clothing laying around the room back into a suitcase. She would buy some new things once she got settled in, she told herself. Then there were the other things she had made a vow to do on this new adventure. One was to get a new bike. She had sold the one she had used for the past ten years to a college student for ten dollars. It was barely worth that much in her estimation, but the young man had insisted. She would buy a nice one and get back into biking, something she had enjoyed in college as exercise and had been her main form of transportation in Tanzania. Yes, she would have to do some research and find just the right cycle. She wanted to use it to get around the neighborhood and maybe for some longer recreational rides.

Jillian also had promised herself a new guitar. The last one she had owned, she left in Africa. She had brought it back with her after her first home leave. Once she paid the "tax" to the crooked airport worker at Kilimanjaro International Airport, she was able to use it to play and sing for those who were suffering in the hospitals and clinics that she served. She also played it in church services. While she and Marty sometimes went to worship at the large, ecumenical church in Arusha, as they got more familiar with the language, they attended a little church with a cement floor and woven walls a few miles out of town. The congregation owned a small electric keyboard, but one never knew if the current would be on that day or not, or whether it would cut out in the middle of a song. An acoustic guitar had been the perfect answer.

Before she and Marty went back to the States, Jillian taught one of their African friends, a fellow church member and good friend named Loi, how to play it and left it with him. She knew he was most likely still playing the same guitar after ten years. People in Tanzania took care of the things they owned like they were the most precious things on earth. They didn't just go out to the store and replace items the second they wanted something new. They didn't waste. They didn't take anything for granted—not food, clothing, possessions, and definitely not their health or their lives. Everything to them was a gift, and they were always thankful for anything that they had.

The bike and the guitar would be easy enough goals to attain, Jillian thought to herself. The other, her third goal, might be more of a challenge. She had told herself that she would begin to date again. And she may even, heaven help her, let herself fall in love again.

Chapter Two

Jillian was in awe as she and Jerry Mack, administrator of Happy Home Housekeeping, drove into the neighborhood where the "client," a Mr. Romano, lived. She hoped that she wasn't gaping like a country girl in the big city for the first time, as that certainly was not the case, but she had never been on her way to *live* in a neighborhood like this one. There was a boulevard lined with neatly spaced palm trees and many gated homes. She wondered if Mr. Romano's house would have a gate. She also wondered what this man did for a living to acquire enough money to live in this neighborhood. She wondered what *any* of these people did to afford such luxury. It certainly wasn't nursing, she thought to herself.

They pulled into a circular driveway, and she was happy that the home was not gated to the street. She didn't want to have to maneuver through a gate every time she wanted to go to or fro, and it also seemed too much for her simple tastes. But her mouth did drop open when she looked ahead. She stared at the huge, two-story "Storybook" design home, as Mr. Mack called it, with its cobblestone walls and uneven roofs. One portion looked like the tower of a castle, with many beautiful windows. Mr. Mack explained that a house built in this style was also referred to as a "fairytale" home, or a "Hansel and Gretel." Right then Jillian felt like she was in a fairy tale—sincerely hoping that it would not end up like Hansel and Gretel.

As magical as it looked, one of her first thoughts was how difficult it was going to be to keep this place clean. All those windows! Those could be a full-time job in themselves. She wondered what was behind them. She would find out soon enough, she guessed.

Mr. Mack slowed to a stop, put the car into park, and turned off the ignition. The two stepped out into the sunshine, as he popped open the trunk with the key fob to retrieve Jillian's luggage. He carried the two suitcases, and she took her laptop case, which also served as her purse for now. He handed her a very large key to the iron gate that led to the back of the property, just to the right of a four-vehicle garage. He informed her that he wanted to make sure she could open the gate. One of the former "helpers," the term the agency preferred to use for their employees, could not open the gate one day and had dared to ring the front doorbell. That was the end of the woman's employment.

Jillian almost asked Mr. Mack if he was joking when he had told her that, but she could tell by the look on his face that he was not. She wondered what kind of person did something like that—fired someone for ringing the doorbell, and Jillian gazed up at the house like it might give her an answer. Out of the corner of her eye, she thought she saw someone looking out from the far left window of the second story, but when she looked again more closely, there was no one there.

She turned her attention to the heavy metal gate and its huge lock. Luckily, she had no problem with the key. She wondered why someone with so much money didn't have a better system for opening the door. As if reading her mind, Mr. Mack apologized for the key, wondering the same thing she had wondered, but guessing that the key seemed more authentic in such a setting. They started down a cobblestone path to the back of the home, adding to Jillian's feeling that she was living a fairy tale.

The backyard was even more breathtaking than the front lawn had been. The sun was shining on a glittering pool, surrounded by a brick patio. There was a small wrought iron table and chair, and a single chaise lounge chair next to them. An elaborate stone grill was at one end of the patio, which looked like it had never been used. A cabana with a dressing room and shower was attached to the back of the house, a large balcony from a second-story room overshadowing it.

The air was filled with the scent of an orange tree laden with ripe fruit, and of roses of various varieties in bloom. It was foreign to Jillian to see flowers at this time of the year. Everything had been covered in two feet of snow when she had left Madison.

They continued past the pool and down a stone path, which cut through a grassy area. Jillian gazed ahead and slightly to her right, where there was an adorable guest cottage also made of cobblestone. It looked like something straight out of the English countryside, and in keeping with the main house, right out of a storybook. She felt the architecture of the property was aptly named.

"Here we are," Mr. Mack said as he gave her the key to open the cottage door. Again, he wanted to make sure she could manage the lock. He certainly didn't need to be bothered, or heaven forbid, Mr. Romano be bothered, if she were to be unable to enter her residence. At least this key seemed to be more regular.

She could barely contain her excitement as she put the key into the lock of her new home. It easily unlocked, and they stepped inside. The main room was well appointed, with a queen-sized bed in black cherry, she thought. There was a desk, dresser, and bureau of the same. Two large, comfortable looking cream-colored overstuffed chairs sat in front of a bay window with a small cherry table between them. A comforter with a delicate flowered pattern on it and pillows of complementary colors and various sizes adorned the bed. The walls and woodwork were painted a lighter shade of cream, providing a bright and cheery ambience. The only thing that didn't fit the English cottage scenario was the flat-screen TV mounted on the wall above the desk and the DVD player and satellite box on the desktop.

They inched their way back through the cottage, Mr. Mack explaining each nook and cranny like a tour guide. Apparently he had had a lot of practice showing it, which made Jillian a bit wary. To her left was a large, deep closet with hangers. She was happy to see those as she had none with her. To her right was a generous-sized bathroom with a double sink, granite countertop, and walk-in shower with brass fixtures and a clear glass door. There was a small closet filled with soft-looking cream-colored towels, a change of sheets, and an extra blanket.

Next was a small kitchenette with stone countertops and stainless steel appliances. "Mr. Romano has had a few food items stocked in your refrigerator and cupboards, seeing that you are arriving on the New Year's Day holiday and may not have the opportunity to go shopping," Mr. Mack informed her. Jillian felt encouraged by this thoughtful gesture. Maybe this man wasn't so bad after all.

There were two stools at the counter. It reminded her of a little pub she had once visited in England. She and her daughter traveled extensively during her work leaves and her daughter's school breaks every year, making the most of their time on the other side of the "pond," as the English called the Atlantic Ocean. By the time they returned to the States, they had visited much of Europe, several other African nations, Greece, Israel, and Turkey.

Next to the kitchenette was an area with a small table for two, a love seat, and a small cherrywood table with a Tiffany reading lamp on it. A sliding door led from the kitchen/dining/living area to a small brick patio where two wrought-iron chairs surrounded a small table. She couldn't help but think of the lone chair at the small table back near the swimming pool. It made her feel sad for a moment, but that feeling didn't last long.

I can live with this, Jillian thought to herself. It was most likely the nicest place she had ever resided, in terms of quality craftsmanship and furnishings. They returned to the kitchen area, and Mr. Mack sat down at the small kitchen table with her, pulling out a pamphlet. "These are your instructions for the care of Mr. Romano's home. Included are days and times for cleaning each room or area as well as a menu for each day with recipes/instructions included." She would prepare one meal per day for Mr. Romano and leave it in the refrigerator, according to the pamphlet. She thought this was odd, but then this whole deal was a bit on the odd side.

"And then there's the cat," he said with a sigh. Jillian had told him before that she had no allergies, so she wasn't sure what the problem could be. "The cat is Mr. Romano's pride and joy. He takes her every Monday morning to the pet store to buy her special food. Mr. Romano feeds her. She is never to be fed anything other than her special food, in case you were to think of giving her a treat." Apparently this had happened once with a helper, and the cat had gotten sick. The helper was terminated, of course. He continued, "Her litter box is to be changed every weekday. And whatever you do, try to avoid contact with the beast. Usually that is not a problem, as Mr. Romano keeps her with him at all times, but every once in a while there has been an—encounter."

"Such as?" Jillian asked, trying to conjure up an image of this vicious feline. She had always liked cats. Her family had many of them on their small farm. Some of the barn cats were pretty wild until they got to know people. They had also had at least one cat in the house at all times. At one point, they had had a dog and two cats residing in their home. She and Marty had gotten a kitten when they had come back to the States. Her name was "Sunny," and she had lived to be eleven years old. She had had a disposition to match her name. Again, Jillian couldn't quite imagine what the big deal was with this particular animal.

Mr. Mack continued, "There have been some pretty nasty scratches, some ruined clothing, and one bite. Then again, the helper in that instance did hit the cat with a broom. If it hadn't been for that fact, Mr. Romano and his cat may have been in trouble." Jillian couldn't imagine hitting any animal with a broom, especially a small one like a cat. "Mostly," Mr. Mack continued, "there are reports of hissing, spitting, and hair-raising growling." He paused. "I hope I haven't frightened you away, Ms. Johnson."

Mr. Mack had obviously never been a nurse, Jillian thought to herself. He was not taking into account Jillian's past experiences in the least. Over the years she had been spit at, scratched, and growled at—by people—numerous times, not to mention the swearing and other hurtful comments that would often fly out of people's mouths when their health was compromised and their worlds were out of normal orbit and control. Nursing was not for the faint of heart in any respect.

If Mr. Mack had said anything else at that moment, she didn't hear it. She was remembering her final nursing rotation in the Intensive Care Unit (ICU) her senior year of college. There was a patient, a young mother, whose lungs had been scarred by an adult case of chicken pox. She had been put on a ventilator in order to breathe, but was conscious. Every time a nurse or therapist came to work with her, she slapped at the person, and not just some little tap either but a real whack. Jillian had been the recipient of quite of few slaps from this woman. Usually it was on her hands as she reached out to change a dressing or check the equipment, but one day she caught it right in the face.

She had held it together in front of the patient, making herself concentrate as hard as she could on the job she had come in to do. But when she was finished, she hurried to the nurse's break room where she burst into tears. Her clinical supervisor, Carol, came in to talk with her, and together they processed the situation. Her supervisor had told her, "Hurt people often hurt people. That young woman has three young children at home. She wants to be there with them, taking care of them, having them drive her crazy, like a normal mom in a normal family situation. Instead, she's lying here helplessly in the ICU because she caught a childhood disease from one of her own kids."

Jillian knew the woman's story. She had had an unusually severe case, even developing pox on her lungs, and they were scarred permanently. The doctors were trying to figure out how to enable her to breathe on her own again, but were fearful that they may not achieve that goal.

Carol continued, "Her husband is at wit's end at home between work, going to the hospital every day, and trying to take care of the kids and the house. Between hospital bills and their loss of income, the family is coming close to financial ruin. That's why she slapped you the way she did. Not because of anything you ever did to her, but because you were there. She can't even swear or scream the way she wants to right now. She is a very frustrated, unhappy, and hurt person, and you were the scapegoat for that frustration, unhappiness, and hurt today."

Jillian's supervisor taught her that day that when someone becomes ill, especially gravely, they suffered great loss, and people were going to take that loss out in some way—somehow—on someone. Often that someone was a person who was there to help them, which seemed unfair, but that was usually the way it played out.

Jillian had learned more from that incident, and from that supervisor, than any one other event or person she encountered in nursing. The supervisor became Jillian's main mentor, and years later a long-time friend and colleague. Carol changed Jillian's perspective that day. Since then, Jillian learned to put herself in other people's shoes. She also learned to answer meanness with kindness, frowns with smiles, and frustration with patience. Of course, there were still times when she became tearful, angry, and even resentful. At those times, she prayed for a patient and understanding heart. And most of the time, Jillian thought, it helped. Jillian was thinking she might have to continue with that strategy in her new job as well, and she supposed it was probably a good practice for life in general.

"Ms. Johnson, are you with me?" asked Mr. Mack. Jillian snapped back to the business at hand. "Now, as to Mr. Romano, he does not like to see the helpers—*at all*. You will find that, if you stay on schedule, that should not be a problem. He also likes to leave notes quite often, usually on the kitchen counter, if there is something else he wants you to do or know about. Finally, if there is a problem of any sort, such as an emergency involving Mr. Romano, please call my office first, and then my cell phone if that is unsuccessful. If for some reason you cannot reach me and need to contact someone, here is the number of Mr. Romano's nephew in Chicago. I am not certain what he could do to help from that distance, but it is the best I can do. It is the only emergency contact number I have in my possession in this case. Do you have any questions?" he asked as he closed the pamphlet and put in down on the table.

Jillian shook her head. "You begin tomorrow morning," Mr. Mack continued. "Thank you, Ms. Johnson, for accepting this assignment." His words sounded to Jillian like they were out of an episode of *Mission Impossible*. "I will contact you in a few days to see how things are going."

They both stood up at the same time. There was a look of pity on the man's face, which he tried to hide unsuccessfully. He closed the door to the cottage behind him and began the trek back through the yard to the gate.

Jillian looked at the pamphlet—actually it was more like a small book. "Looks like I have some homework to do," she said aloud to herself. She decided to sit out on the patio to do her studying. She found a glass in the cupboard and filled it with water and carried it to the small iron table.

The chair scraped the brick as she moved it back, and again as she pulled it forward up to the table. She set the book down and started to read. She found herself laughing after a page or two. She remembered how often she and other nurses would have to laugh at some of the ridiculous situations that came up, things they were asked to do, or difficult people that needed to be dealt with. Even though it didn't change a situation, a little levity could help change one's attitude.

As she read the numerous lists of do's and don'ts, she thought that this man must be mad. Or perhaps a kinder, more adequate description might be eccentric. She never had asked Mr. Mack what Mr. Romano did—correction, had done—for a living. It must be something rather important. She had had to sign a confidentiality form when she was first offered the position, saying that she would not discuss things she saw or heard in this house outside of this house, but she had assumed this was standard operating procedure in all homes. She was used to treating people and situations in a confidential manner, so it was not a new or big deal to her. She figured he was probably one of those computer geniuses or a scientist who invented something special. That must be how he made enough money to own this property.

She went to the last page again of the book again, where the emergency contact information was printed. Who was this Mr. Romano? Maybe she could Google him tonight and get some perspective on him.

She saw the nephew's name and address, Thomas A. Romano, Libertyville, Illinois, and his phone numbers on the top of the page. On the bottom of the page was information in case there was a medical emergency or fire and she would need to give the physical address for the property. Her heart stopped as she read the following: "address for John D. Romano…" She didn't get any further than the name.

She reread the name again, then just stared at it. She felt the years melt away. Suddenly she was that 19-year-old sitting on the sofa in the dorm lounge on a Thursday evening again, waiting for her favorite show—*O.R.*, starring John D. Romano and Monica Morgan, the show that had led her to medical school, which led to Marty, which led to the life she had lived ever since her daughter was born twenty-five years ago. Her head was swimming with a million thoughts and feelings, and she had to take some deep breaths. "What is going on?" she asked quietly and looked upward as if hoping for an answer.

She sat blankly for an unknown amount of time, unable to function. She was so surprised, or maybe stunned was a better word. She looked at her watch. What time was it in Senegal? She needed to talk to her daughter—now.

She dialed up Marty but didn't get an answer. In the meantime, she did some meditation techniques she had used in many of her work settings over the years to help calm patients or sometimes herself if needed. With each deep breath she inhaled, she felt herself becoming more centered and relaxed. Now maybe she could process the situation more calmly.

What was the big deal anyway? She wasn't even going to see this guy. Mr. Romano. Mr. John D. Romano, the actor whom she had found so attractive so many years ago. The person whose girlfriend on and off the show had made her want to become a cardiac surgeon. The reason she… She was doing it again, and she felt herself getting more and more wound up. She took a few more breaths.

He wouldn't even know she was there. In fact, he didn't even want to know that she was there. He wouldn't know her story. He knew nothing of a college girl with a celebrity crush, or her wanting to go to medical school to become a surgeon like his girlfriend on his popular show, or that when she went to medical school she made some decisions that changed the course of her life forever. He didn't, and wouldn't, know any of it. So, again, she asked herself, what was the big deal? She guessed that she was just surprised to have a piece of her past thrown into her present.

She decided she needed to eat something. That, and get some air. She checked to see what Mr. Romano had stocked for her. There was an incredible-looking loaf of whole grain bread in the cupboard, so if there was nothing else, she would be content. It looked like comfort food, and right now, she was in need of some comfort. There were two types of all-natural jams in the cupboard, along with jars of organic peanut butter and honey, and two kinds of soup. Fruits, cheeses, a salad mix, and some eggs, all labeled as organic, occupied the refrigerator. The man was into healthy foods at least. She noticed that most of his recipes in "the book," as she had come to think of it, were for healthy items, so at least he must still care about something in this world, like good physical health. The description and floor plan map of the house also showed a rather large workout room. She wondered if it was ever used, but would find out soon enough.

She carried a plate with a peanut butter and honey sandwich, along with a bottle of green tea, out to the little patio. There was a quart of milk in the refrigerator, but she would use that sparingly until she could get to a store. She would have to buy more soon. She was from "America's Dairyland," after all.

Jillian sat at the table outside and continued to read through "the book," which she held on her lap. She made notes for the next day on a pad of paper she had brought with her. She didn't want to lose her job in record time because she made some silly mistake. She would play this "game"—at least for now. Jillian was curious about what was going on in this man's life that was making him so regimented, rigid, and cut off from the rest of the world, including his family.

After she devoured her dinner, she washed the dishes and headed for the bed. It turned out to be the most comfortable bed she had ever sat upon. She couldn't help making a comparison between this place and the hotel room where she had spent the better part of the past week. Actually, she thought, there was no comparison.

She opened up her laptop and typed the name—John D. Romano—into the search engine. She could not believe all the references that popped up on the screen. After about an hour of reading every kind of nonsense imaginable, she decided to give it a rest. She wondered how any normal human being could put up with such garbage. There were a few reasonable, generic informational articles—the kind that gave a short personal history, talked about what roles he played on what TV show, play, or movie, and the dates for those performances. But for every one of those, there were several of the more bizarre variety. One said that John D. Romano was no longer living. One said he had relapsed into his prescription drug addiction after twenty years and was living on a commune near San Francisco. Another said he was living at a monastery in Tibet! Jillian wondered how people came up with these things.

There were photos of John D. Romano, smiling while holding an award or a beautiful woman. Many photos were with Monica Morgan, but there were other gorgeous women as well. And then there were photos of his unhappy face, with captions below them with allegations and gossip of every sort. No wonder the man was depressed. At least she thought he sounded depressed to her.

She decided she wasn't going to solve anything that evening, if ever. She tried Marty one more time, unsuccessfully, so emailed her instead to set up a video-chat date for one of the next several evenings. Right now she was going to get unpacked, take a shower, and go to bed. She wanted to get up bright and early for her new adventure. If she had thought it was an adventure before this latest development, she now thought it had the makings of a grand escapade. She couldn't wait to talk to Marty about it and wondered what her reaction would be.

The hot shower, with the shower head that reminded her of a huge sunflower, seemed to melt away much of her tension and trepidation. She crawled between the cool sheets of her bed, turned off the lamp next to it, and decided to do one last thing before she went to sleep—what she usually did every night. She prayed for her daughter, her friends that she missed, and anyone in need. She also said the prayer she usually said when she was a nurse. She asked that God would help her be a helper to others. As she said that, it suddenly dawned on her—that is what the agency called their house workers—helpers. That brought a smile to her face and a certain kind of peace to her heart. And before she shut her eyes, she said one last prayer—for John D. Romano.

Chapter Three

Jillian awakened early the next morning to an unfamiliar sound. She had always been a notoriously light sleeper, which she admitted came in handy as a single mom and as a nurse. She heard every minute sound her daughter made in her sleep. At work, she often baffled her colleagues when she could hear a patient cough or whisper for help before the person could even reach the nurse's call button. "How do you do that, Jillian?" they would often ask. "You really could hear a pin drop, couldn't you?" She would answer with a shrug of her shoulders.

The sound came from outside. It was some kind of splashing sound. Then she remembered that there was a pool only a short distance from her current residence. But it was only six a.m. and not even light yet. And it was January. Sure, it was Southern California, but still, it couldn't be much more than fifty-five degrees out there. Would Mr. Romano really be swimming? Then again, she thought, she had read that he grew up in northern Illinois. Maybe he was like the male students she would see on campus, who wore shorts to class the minute the thermometer rose above the freezing mark.

She decided to get up and investigate. Her alarm was set to go off soon anyway. She didn't care to wake up twice in one day, so it wasn't worth trying to go back to sleep. She reached over and turned off her cell phone alarm and threw back the covers. She paused a moment, sitting up on the edge of the bed, instinctively checking for messages or emails from Marty. There were no new ones. She laid the phone down, rose, and walked over to the bay window. She peeked out and saw a dim light shining in the cabana. She couldn't see who was in the pool, but there were not a whole lot of options.

At the thought of being seen by her employer, Jillian suddenly backed away from the window. She walked to the kitchenette and made some coffee. There was a small bag of fair trade beans in the cupboard, a coffee grinder, and a small French press. She heated some water in the microwave and poured it into the press, put the top on, and gently pressed down on the plunger.

After finding a sharp knife in a drawer, she sliced a grapefruit in half and toasted a piece of the fantastic bread from the day before. She was going to have to find out where that came from. It was a "keeper," as she and her daughter would say when they tried a new food or recipe that they really enjoyed. She spread the Marion blackberry jam on her toast, and her breakfast was complete.

When she had finished eating and cleaning up, she found herself again drawn to the window. She stood much further back this time, as dawn was breaking. She peered out just in time to see a well-muscled body rising up out of the steamy pool. He grabbed a large white towel off the back of the chaise lounge and started walking toward the cabana. There was the familiar limp, but otherwise Mr. Romano appeared to be in fantastic physical condition. The answer to her question about whether the exercise room was ever used was answered by the broad shoulders and lean body she had just observed. His body looked like it belonged to someone twenty years younger. If it hadn't been for the mostly gray hair, one would never guess this man was almost sixty, at least according to the Internet. But considering his fit body, she noticed that he walked slowly, with his shoulders slumped forward a bit. There was an air of dejection about him, even in the freshness of a new morning. She drew herself away from the window, suddenly feeling like a "Peeping Tom."

Jillian showered, loving the powerful stream of soft water. It was nothing like the stingy shower in their small farmhouse growing up—"hard water and low water pressure out in the country," her father would say whenever she complained. And this was definitely not like the makeshift showers, or baths out of a plastic baby bathtub with water that had been heated over a wood fire, that she encountered in Africa. The towels made her feel like royalty and were as soft and luxurious as they looked. *You're going to get spoiled if you stay here too long.*

She put on her work clothes (khaki slacks and a black long-sleeved T-shirt from Lands' End) and headed to the main house. She couldn't wait to see the inside. She had studied the floor plan and was impressed. She especially could not wait to visit the library—the room with the many windows—but that wouldn't happen until the next day.

Her first stop was the kitchen. She ran her hand across the smooth semi-precious stone countertop. She would have to make certain to check out the care and maintenance of this one, she thought. It was a beautiful surface, and very expensive, she perceived correctly. On the corner of the high countertop, which had stools below it, was a huge cube of self-stick notes with a pen next to them. She checked the pad to see if there was any writing on it, but it was blank. Mr. Mack had told her that if there were any communications from Mr. Romano, they would come in the form of notes.

The kitchen was a pleasant, spacious room with an eat-in breakfast nook. She immediately loved this room, but then again, she loved kitchens in general. Even the simple "summer kitchens" outside the main houses in Tanzania had been some of her favorite places. Kitchens were where people gathered together, cooked together, talked, and in her house growing up, said prayers around the table before a home-cooked meal.

She remembered her kitchen on the farm. Her dad would take a break between his day job and going out to do the evening chores, which consisted of feeding the small herd of steers and a few chickens that they raised. He would sit on a chair next to the kitchen stove, dressed in his dark green work clothes, while her mom started dinner—usually something made with beef. Jillian would sit on her dad's lap, even into her early teens, and the three of them discussed their "days" with one another. It was one of her favorite times of the day, and one of her best memories of her childhood.

Her mind refocused on the task at hand. She looked over "the book" and her notes from the night before, and got to work. Her first task was to empty the trash from the kitchen into the receptacle in the garage and then wheel the container to the end of the driveway. It was trash day.

She checked off the chores, one by one, making certain she hadn't missed anything, and kept a close watch on the clock to make sure she wasn't "sighted" by her employer. She wondered what Mr. Romano would think if he knew *he* had been sighted by her that morning. The image of him standing there dripping wet in his swimsuit entered her mind, but it left quickly as she threw herself into a fervent cleaning of the refrigerator and kitchen sink.

The end of the workday came quickly. Jillian had always enjoyed days that were busy at the hospital, especially if it was routine busyness, and not an emergency scenario. Just before 4:30 p.m., she put the lentil stew she had made, exactly according to the directions, into the refrigerator. Left to her own tastes, she would have put more spices in it and added some cut-up kale, but it wasn't her place to change anything—at least she wasn't daring enough to do anything like that yet, if ever. She left the sunny kitchen and headed back through the yard, past the pool, and down the short path to the cottage.

A shopping list was top priority. Jillian sat outside, enjoying the last of the daylight and warmth as she wrote, then called a taxi for a visit to the nearest grocery store. When she returned home, she poured herself a tall glass of fat-free milk and made a rice dish, pilau, that she and Marty had learned how to make in Africa. It was their favorite meal. She had forgotten how large a quantity it made, however, and her small refrigerator and freezer were pretty full after her journey to the store. She stared at all the food. There was no way she could finish all of it by herself, even if she was good at eating leftovers. Maybe she could share some with Mr. Romano, she thought. She always enjoyed it when someone made something for her. She would take some along with her the next day and leave it in the refrigerator.

❖

If Mr. Romano had gone swimming the next morning, Jillian didn't hear him. Instead, she woke to the chirping of her cell phone alarm. Turning her thoughts to the day ahead, she felt excitement. Today was "library day." She was curious about Mr. Romano's book collection. She tried to imagine it as she got ready for the day.

Once in the main house, she stopped in the kitchen to drop off the extra pilau on the way to her first assignment for the day—the mini-theater, which looked like a room no one ever used when she entered it. She worked quickly, but realized that she had to stay on schedule, so she slowed her pace.

When the appointed time came to enter the library, her jaw dropped. She knew schools and even some small town libraries that would covet the collection, which contained the classics of literature, many expensively bound. She remembered reading that Mr. Romano had studied literature at Northwestern University. Apparently he had had a number of colleges recruiting him for football, but he had chosen Northwestern over other schools because of its tough academics. This man sounded very intelligent, and his library bore credence to that.

In the last game of John Romano's junior football season, he sustained a career-ending injury, and from the sound of it to Jillian, a botched surgery on his knee. The nurse in her wondered if he had ever gone in for a "consult" now that there were so many advancements in that area. He had been the starting quarterback for the team, and there were rumors that he might be good enough to play professionally after graduation.

Jillian thought about how quickly something could happen in life to change the course of one's history. *One moment you think you're going to play in the NFL, the next one you are undergoing surgery and rethinking your options. One moment you think you are going to be a cardiac surgeon, the next one you are a nurse and a mother.*

Because John Romano was a 4.0 student, he received an academic scholarship to finish his senior year, as he no longer had an athletic scholarship. But from what she had also read, she wasn't so sure he was too sad about his injury in the long run, other than the physical pain and subsequent struggle with prescription pain killers it caused.

After football, he discovered acting, or it discovered him. He got the lead in the first college play for which he auditioned the spring after his injury, and again in every subsequent show during his senior year. He was as natural on stage as he was on the football field. He tried the New York theater scene after graduation, but a friend convinced him to give Los Angeles a shot. The rest, as is often said, is history.

Jillian gazed around the mahogany shelves again. Not only was she awed by the books, but inside a glass case were two Emmy and three Golden Globe Awards. She had never seen either in real life, only on the television screen. They were stunning. Next to one of the statues was a photo of Mr. Romano, smiling from ear to ear, and holding the award. Equally stunning, she thought. He looked so very happy. She wished that somehow he could be happy like that again.

She finished her dusting, dust mopping the floor, and general straightening. If she could have, she would have loved to plunk herself down in the comfortable chair with the high-powered reading lamp next to it. She dusted the mahogany table on the other side of the chair, moving a pair of reading glasses, a telephone, and an expensive-looking edition of *Tess of the d'Urbervilles*, Mr. Romano's apparent current read. No wonder the man was depressed. She and Marty had both loved, and hated, that book. She and her daughter had read many books out loud to each other over the years in Tanzania, as there was no television. Even after they returned to the U.S., they continued this practice. When they read *Tess*, time and time again they hoped she would catch a break, but the storyline went in the opposite direction. There were no fairytale endings in that tome.

Jillian finished polishing the table and a desk in the room. She had been ecstatic to learn that she was not responsible for the windows. Apparently a service had been procured to do that.

She used a rolling library ladder to reach and dust the highest shelves. When she was done dusting and admiring each new title she discovered, she climbed down the ladder and looked one last time around the impressive room.

The library was done for today. She reluctantly took her cleaning supplies and closed the door to the room behind her. She decided on her way back to the kitchen that she needed to find a public library soon, and hopefully a book club. She felt inspired and needed books to read. She needed to meet new friends.

In the kitchen, she made Mr. Romano's requested meal, exactly as printed. She thought that eventually she would try to put in a few subtle changes here and there and see what happened. She might not be a trained chef, but she was known as a good cook and she enjoyed cooking and baking. She put the food in the refrigerator, noticing the pilau she had brought over earlier that morning. She figured she shouldn't leave it in the plastic container from the cottage kitchen. She looked through the cupboards and retrieved a pretty china serving dish and spooned the food onto it. She covered it with clear plastic wrap and put it back into the refrigerator. Then she wrote a note to Mr. Romano on a sheet of paper from the cube on the counter.

Your meal is prepared as you requested. I also left some other food I thought you might enjoy. If you do not care for the dish, please feel free to throw it away.

❖

That night Jillian had plans to get back to her blog. She had written several posts since this whole adventure had begun. The first one had been written back in the hotel, which discussed how to know when to make a change in your life and examining the motives for that change. She had confessed that her current move was, for the first time in her experience, not precipitated by some kind of personal crisis. She wasn't running away from something this time. Instead, she felt like she was running *to* something—she just didn't know what that something was for certain. She invited others to talk about any changes going on in their lives and to discuss what prompted them.

Her second post was written the previous night, after her first day on the job—and after recovering from the surprise of learning that her employer had a connection to her past. Of course, she had no intention of discussing any particulars in this case.

Kathy J. Jacobson

Instead, she engaged in a discourse about triggers—things that bring on memories—for example, running into a person, hearing a song, smelling a scent, visiting a special place—things that bring the past into the present.

Jillian admitted that often her initial response in such situations was to block out the memories. Now she felt that the best thing was to face them, to feel them, to heal them, and to start making new memories. Better ones. The post had generated a lot of feedback and an outpouring of others' stories. Some thanked her for sharing her thoughts and said they would give "facing, feeling, and healing" a try the next time they encountered a trigger situation.

But before she got to go "home" for the day and start blogging, Jillian had one more assignment—the workout room. It, like the library, was state-of-the-art. It could have rivaled many high-priced fitness centers. Her job was to wipe down each piece of equipment. As Jillian moved the cloth over the metal, she thought about how often these machines were used, based on the way her employer had looked.

The idea that she had even noticed that made her blush, but it also made her think that perhaps this was a healthy sign. Maybe she was finally returning from the dead, a word one of her friends back home had boldly told her was an accurate description of her love life. For many—too many—years, she wouldn't let herself even *think* about a man. These new thoughts made Jillian consider the possibility that sometime in this new year, she might really be ready for goal number three on her list, after all. Now she just needed to get out and begin meeting some people in her new locale, or chances of that would be nil.

Those thoughts prompted the subject of her blog post that night. She asked others to share their own experiences of stepping away and then getting back into the dating/relationship scene. It seemed everyone had stories of withdrawing from love for a time, even from the love of family and friends, when they were bro-kenhearted. They shared their thoughts about risking love again, both the good and the bad.

Jillian was really enjoying the blog, much more than she had anticipated. She had forgotten how good it felt to share one's feel-ings with others and to have their support. Her goal had been to help others with her blog, but she was certain that she was ben-efiting just as much as her readers were, and maybe even more.

She felt uplifted after writing that evening, but then her mind turned back to Mr. Romano. She wondered if he had anyone with whom to share his thoughts and feelings. She thought about what Mr. Mack had told her about him the first time they had met in his office. He said that Mr. Romano does not take calls from any-one, even his nephew. He wasn't working at the present time. He didn't even want to *see* the help, let alone talk to them. She felt bad for him, but she also didn't want to pity him. If he was anything like her, pity was the last thing he wanted or needed from other people. But he did need something. She just didn't know what that something was, or even if she did, what she could possibly do about it.

Jillian finished getting ready for bed, and looked out the win-dow one last time at a huge moon. It was one of those "man in the moon" kind of moons, and she seemed to direct her prayers in its direction. She thanked God for new opportunities. She prayed for her daughter and for her important work fighting Ebola. She prayed for her friends in many places, and that she would find some new friends in her current surroundings. Then she went into her usual—that she would be a helper, whether it be through her blog or some other way. And lastly, she prayed for her employ-er. She closed the blinds and crawled into the cozy bed, drifting off to sleep with a good feeling in her heart.

Chapter Four

Jillian's good feeling disappeared quickly the next morning. She went into the kitchen of the main house, not even thinking about the pilau she had left the day before for Mr. Romano. Her mind was on the fact that she was going to clean five bathrooms that day. She had thought that was bad enough, but then she read the note from Mr. Romano that was waiting for her on the counter. It was a simple sentence.

I didn't care for the "dish."

So, he hadn't liked the rice dish. Not everyone enjoyed that type of food, so she could understand that. She opened the refrigerator, thinking she could always take it home with her, wishing she had left it in the plastic container. The dish wasn't there. He must have thrown out the food, washed the dish and put it away, she thought. But that wasn't the case either, as she found when she checked the cupboard. She checked all the other cupboards as well, but the dish was nowhere in sight. *What in the world happened to it?* She stood thinking and wondering for a moment. *He wouldn't.*

She opened the drawer to the slide-out garbage container and there it was—the pilau—still in the beautiful china dish with the clear wrap over it—the entire thing in the garbage. *Why would anyone do such a thing?*

Jillian was angry at first. She took a few deep breaths and calmed down. She started going through that same process she had done with every difficult patient she had dealt with over the years since that first slap in the face. She put herself in his shoes, although in this case, she wasn't sure exactly what that was all about. She told herself that he was not a healthy person right now, for whatever reason. He was unhappy. He was hurt.

As usual, this ritual helped her, and she gently retrieved the dish from the garbage. She put the rice down the garbage disposal, thinking of the people she personally knew who didn't have enough food to eat on a regular basis. There had been so much malnourishment in Tanzania. Even in the city of Milwaukee, there were many hungry people. Throwing away food was one of her least favorite things to do in the world. That was what had prompted her wanting to share it in the first place—not to be wasteful. She was also trying to be nice. She guessed it hadn't been the greatest idea after all.

After washing and drying the dish, she put it away where she had found it the day before. She tied up the trash bag, lifted it out of the bin, and took it out to the garage. She opened the large, wheeled trash receptacle and was just about to toss in the bag of when something inside caught her eye. It looked like a book. It *was* a book. For the second time that morning, she felt stunned and confused. Why would Mr. Romano throw out a book? From what she knew about his studies and from the looks of his library, he revered them.

She looked around her to make sure she was alone. She tilted the bin and fished out the book. It was a copy of Monica Morgan's new autobiography, *Golden Girl*. There she was on the cover, still looking amazing. Monica looked like she was a decade younger than her actual age, but then again, so did Jillian. She wondered what Monica's secret was. She attributed her own appearance to healthy eating, exercising, faith, and raising only one very low-maintenance child who was the joy of her life.

Monica was smiling widely with her full lips and perfect teeth. She was wearing her Olympic gold medal around her neck and clasping her Emmy Award in one hand and an Academy Award in the other. She still had long, silky golden locks, although Jillian wasn't certain whether the color was real or out of a bottle. Maybe Monica was fortunate, like she was, as Jillian had yet to dye her hair.

Again, she wondered what had made Mr. Romano do such a thing. She put the book back exactly as she found it and covered the garbage can. She would have to download the book tonight onto her computer after she talked to her daughter. They had a "date" set up at six p.m. for a video call.

Jillian went about her day's schedule. The bathroom cleaning was not as unpleasant a job as she had feared. The entire house didn't seem very lived in to her. There were a lot of rooms, but there was no one to mess them up, so cleaning was pretty superficial in some areas. It was such a beautiful house, but it didn't feel like a home. It was more like a collection of rooms, with no one enjoying them, no one really *living* in them.

She made Mr. Romano's dinner that night, exactly as prescribed. After the pilau incident, she didn't dare make any deviations. She put the food, a simple chicken recipe, in the refrigerator and turned to the counter. She hadn't planned on it, but she felt compelled to reply to that morning's note from her employer. She wrote just one word, in capital letters, followed by an exclamation point.

NOTED!

She tore the paper off the cube and slapped it down next to Mr. Romano's note from that morning. Maybe she would get fired, but she didn't particularly care at that moment. She closed the kitchen door behind her, harder than she needed to, and headed for her abode.

Once in the cottage, Jillian wearily fell into one of the cream-colored chairs and dozed off, waking up just in time to talk to Marty.

"Hi, Mom!" her daughter said, her smile and upbeat voice pulling Jillian out of her funk. "What's up today?"

She told Marty about the dish of pilau incident. "He *didn't!*" her daughter exclaimed.

Jillian nodded. Then Marty surprised her by beginning to laugh, which started Jillian laughing as well. With the exception of the wasted food aspect, it *was* pretty funny. And the way he put the quotation marks around the word "dish" in his note to her. *Clever*, she had to admit, albeit in a sarcastic sort of way.

She proceeded to tell Marty about the book she had found in the trash and how surprised she was, considering Mr. Romano's adoration of the written word. Her daughter seemed as impressed as her mother had been as Jillian described the incredible selections in the library in the house, and agreed that he didn't seem like the type of person who would throw away a book.

Marty mentioned that perhaps there was something in the book that had put him in a rotten mood, leading him to discard the book—and to dumping of a perfectly good dish full of her favorite food into the garbage. That was the worst part, Marty said, and she exclaimed that she was going to have to make some pilau that night for dinner. She was having a few friends over, and now she knew exactly what she would make. She would tell them about the incident—if that was all right with Jillian —not mentioning any names or places, of course. Jillian told her to "go for it."

They talked for an hour, discussing work and the world, then

Marty needed to go to the hospital. Although it was morning for Marty, she said goodnight to Jillian the same way they had ever since their years in Africa.

"Lala salama, Mama," which was Swahili for "safe sleeping."

It was a nice way to end a day that hadn't been very nice. As always, Jillian felt better after talking to her daughter. She again thought about how blessed she was to be "Mama Marty." In Tanzania, a parent was identified by being either the mother, "Mama," or father, "Baba," of one's firstborn child. Therefore, she was often referred to as "Mama Marty" outside of her professional setting, a title which Jillian adored.

Jillian stood up from the chair, and her stomach growled loudly. She suddenly realized that she hadn't eaten any supper. She walked back to the refrigerator to check out the possibilities. She considered some of the leftover pilau she still had in the refrigerator, but she wasn't sure she could manage to eat it without either laughing herself to death or worrying herself to death about whether or not she would have a job the next morning after Mr. Romano read her note.

She decided to have a bowl of cereal—comfort food to her and what she often ate when nothing really sounded good or she was very tired, both of which were the case that evening. She hoped that she wasn't coming down with something. That tended to happen to her when she got stressed out—and moving, starting a blog and a new job, even if they were things you wanted to do, were major stressors for certain.

She finished the cereal and had some orange juice. The juice was fantastic in Southern California, as was all the year-round fresh produce. She was getting spoiled already, and it had only been a short two weeks since she landed at the airport.

She washed the bowl, spoon, and glass and plopped down on her bed. She decided to download a copy of *Golden Girl* onto her computer and started reading.

The first half of the book talked about Monica Morgan's childhood, her swimming career, and how that led her to an acting career. With her blonde hair, bright blue eyes, model height, out-of-this-world body, and go-getter, winner mentality, she was a natural for the Hollywood scene and had numerous agents pursue her following the Olympics.

Jillian skimmed through the chapters, not seeing anything that she thought would be upsetting to Mr. Romano. Perhaps the issue was the mention of Monica getting a lead role in a movie and landing an Academy Award for it. Jillian had read one Internet article that said Mr. Romano felt he had never achieved greatness in his profession because he had not received an "Oscar."

She got to the chapter about Monica's years on *O.R.* The first part talked about her audition, callbacks, and screen tests. She talked about the wonderful writing on the program. She mentioned her many talented co-stars, ending with her "on-screen love," Dr. Nick Caruso, played by John D. Romano, whom she described as a very talented, serious actor.

Monica went on say that if it hadn't been for *O.R.* she would never have met the "love of her life." Jillian thought for a moment that she must be talking about Mr. Romano, but the narrative continued, "If Ben Bastien hadn't guest-starred during the final season, I would have missed meeting my soulmate." She continued on about how he was everything she had ever wanted in a man—intelligent, strong, sexy, funny, and a real family man. She said that Ben made her laugh every day and described how he loved to play practical jokes. The story continued by describing her fertility problems and then the miraculous birth of their twin sons, who were just turning twenty-two.

Jillian scanned back and forth throughout the book, looking for more references to Mr. Romano, but saw none. Monica Morgan seemed to have completely dismissed their personal relationship. Maybe there really wasn't one, although there were many articles saying that there had been—and a myriad of photos of Monica Morgan and John D. Romano together that sure looked like they were more than just friends and co-workers. Maybe those were just for publicity.

Perhaps Monica's lack of mention of Mr. Romano was just her way of being discreet, as a way to protect their past. But Jillian's guess was that if the book ended up in the garbage can, Mr. Romano didn't see it that way. Jillian decided that she didn't really see it that way either. She knew what it felt like to be dismissed by someone you had once loved. So before she closed her laptop for the night, she hit the delete button on her computer, putting "Golden Girl" in the trash, just like her employer.

Chapter Five

Jillian was astonished when two weeks on the job had already passed. She had been so grateful that she hadn't received a call of dismissal from Mr. Mack, nor was there a note on the counter when she entered the kitchen the morning after the "dish" incident in response to her rash one-word note. She had braced herself for anything, and her eyes had flown to the countertop when she had stepped into the kitchen that day. She had been relieved when it was bare. Actually, there had been no more notes since, which filled Jillian with an odd sense of disappointment.

By this time, Jillian had cleaned every room in the house at least once, and it was time to start the rotation over. There had been no more sightings of Mr. Romano. She made a conscious effort to not look out the window in the early morning when he would take his swims. She couldn't afford to make another mistake. Whether or not she was, she felt like she was on probation, which would be normal for any position. Even if it was self-imposed, Jillian felt it was important, and in her best interest, to set and keep high standards for herself.

There had been no cat sightings during this time either. She cleaned the litter box and the cat's bowls every weekday. She noticed a brush for the cat, and orange fur in the trash each day. Mr. Romano certainly babied this animal. It was surprising that it was supposedly so nasty considering it was meticulously well-cared for.

On the more personal front, Jillian decided after the Monica Morgan book incident to buy the entire series of *O.R.*, a deluxe set of all six years that had just been released on DVD about the same time as Monica's book had hit the stands. For some reason, Jillian felt compelled to watch this show again, which had once been such an integral and influential part of her life. She was a bit fearful of the memories it could unleash, but perhaps that wouldn't be such a bad thing. It could be a part of her facing, feeling, and healing process, she told herself.

She picked up the package containing the DVDs at her post office box the next week. She couldn't wait to start watching them, and once she started watching them, she couldn't stop watching. It was even worse than when she was nineteen. She thought it was a good thing they hadn't had DVDs of shows back then, or she may have flunked out of nursing school.

Jillian was obsessed—or maybe a better word was possessed. She knew the series had been ground-breaking. She knew the writing was outstanding. But she had forgotten how many subjects they had covered and how accurate they were most of the time. The writers had certainly done their homework.

It also reminded Jillian of how much medicine had changed since that show began. Procedures were now so much more advanced. Things that people on the show routinely died from were now routinely cured. Another big change was the privacy issue. No one would ever be able to discuss cases so openly or share patient information today.

The thing that impressed Jillian the most was how accurately the emotional aspects of working in the medical field—the stress, the victories and the heartaches, the interactions and relationships between doctors and nurses and other staff members—were portrayed, and how relevant they still were.

It also gave a realistic view of how difficult life could be for the doctors and nurses who did not have good support systems at home. If one's significant other didn't understand the world of a medical professional, it often caused problems and ended many relationships. Jillian figured that was why so many people were attracted to one another within the profession. They needed someone in their personal life to *understand*. She imagined that was most likely true in many other professions as well, but she knew it was of utmost importance in the medical field.

Jillian was still amazed when she watched the romances on the series. The show really "pushed the envelope" in that area. Her mom would have called many of the scenes "steamy," especially for television in the '80s. The scenes between Dr. Nick Caruso and Dr. Pamela Prine were especially, for lack of a better term, *realistic*. The two actors had quite the onscreen chemistry, and she found it difficult to believe that it hadn't carried over into the real lives of John D. Romano and Monica Morgan.

They made a stunning couple. Their characters were so intelligent. She remembered now why she wanted to be Dr. Prine. And they were so attractive. And even though she had only seen Mr. Romano early one morning in semi-darkness and Monica Morgan on the cover of a book, *they still are*, she thought.

Jillian watched the program every evening for the next three weeks. She sat on her bed transfixed. She began to add an exercise routine while watching the program, not even taking time for her usual walks. As soon as she was done watching the series, she *had* to buy herself a bicycle.

Marty sent her a message on social media, worried that something was wrong when she hadn't heard from Jillian in a week. She told Marty about the series and some of her observations about it.

Marty asked her to keep the DVDs for her to watch when she returned from her rotation. She would like to see the show someday, especially since it was in some way a part of her story, too.

Jillian was so preoccupied with the show that she didn't notice that *she* was being sighted. She hadn't closed her blinds yet for the evening, so now it was Mr. Romano's turn to watch Jillian. From his balcony on the second floor over the cabana, he watched as she sat mesmerized on her bed, watching a piece of *his* very own past on the television screen.

❖

The last season of *O.R.* was the most difficult one for Jillian to watch. She realized by the dates on the DVD box that it coincided with the year she became pregnant, had her heart shattered, gave up on a dream, and went home humiliated. The memories and feelings came flooding back like a river in spring after the snow melts.

"How could you not have taken precautions?" That was what Jeffrey—Dr. Jeffrey A. Lawrence—had asked her when she told him she was pregnant. It was funny that he hadn't been concerned with that when they went to his apartment supposedly to talk about her research paper six weeks before.

"How do I know that it's even mine?"

"Jeffrey, I've never been with anyone else but you—ever," Jillian had answered, stunned by his accusatory tone and question.

"You expect me to believe that in this day and age?" he went on.

"It's the truth."

"What do you want?" he asked.

"What do you mean?" Jillian asked. In her heart, she was saying *for you to say you love me, the baby, and want to get married.*

"Are you looking for an "A" in this class or a favor on your internship—or money?" he continued, his words like fingernails on the chalkboard of Jillian's heart.

She couldn't even speak. She began to cry.

"Oh, sure. Now you're crying. You've gotten yourself into a predicament and want me to solve it for you. I know it's not legal in this state, but I have a friend in another who could help you out..."

"You mean an abortion?" Jillian asked.

"A procedure, let's call it," he said with a smirk. Jillian wondered who this person was standing in front of her. Where was the brilliant, revered doctor and professor? Where was the "Mr. Nice Guy" she had fallen in love with, who had sweet-talked her into his bed and into forgetting herself six weeks ago?

Perhaps it was because she had parents who had waited forever to have a child or because of the way she was raised in general, but she just couldn't consider an abortion as an option. All of a sudden, she had felt herself getting angry. She picked up her books and research paper and turned to the good professor.

"Goodbye, Dr. Lawrence," Jillian said. Those were the last words she ever spoke to the father of her child. She withdrew from medical school the next morning, booked a flight to the Midwest, and flew home the day after that. Luckily, her roommates found someone to sublet her room in their apartment immediately. It was a sought-after commodity in a great location. At least she had made the right decision in one area of her life. Everything else, it felt to her, was a complete mistake.

❖

Another thing that pained Jillian as she watched that final season of *O.R.* were the episodes with Ben Bastien, Monica Morgan's husband of now almost twenty-five years. He had guest-starred as a heart specialist Dr. James, who had come to lecture and work with the heart team on the show over several episodes. In the script, the writers had Dr. Pamela Prine and Dr. Nick Caruso going through a rough patch in their relationship, and Dr. James taking advantage of the situation by asking Dr. Prine out on a date. She had hesitated, but after an argument with Dr. Caruso, she reconsidered, and they had gone to dinner at a five-star restaurant. Dr. James continued to pursue her in the show, but the writers decided that the fans would not be happy about a break-up of their favorite couple, so of course, Dr. Prine and Dr. Caruso, came out fine in the end—on the show at least.

Jillian could see it in his eyes after those guest-star episodes were over. Those beautiful brown eyes of John D. Romano, which had often looked like they were sparkling, especially when he looked at Dr. Prine/Monica Morgan. They looked dulled with pain. The twinkle was gone, and there was a subtle sadness about them.

Monica Morgan had said in her autobiography that if Ben Bastien hadn't come on the show in the final season, she would have missed meeting the "love of her life." It was clear to Jillian that Mr. Romano had thought of himself as the "love of her life," but he had found out differently. He, like Jillian, had suffered a great hurt during that final season. Jillian may have never officially met him, but their lives had been on a parallel course once, at least in matters of the heart. She couldn't really explain it, but as she put the last DVD back into its case, she again felt oddly connected to John D. Romano.

Chapter Six

Now that Jillian was done watching *O.R.* and had her life back, she got on track with her plans. She had managed to find a church and a public library over the last month. She still hadn't found a book club, but admittedly hadn't put much effort into it once she had become glued to the television set.

Jillian still hadn't purchased a bike either, and she really wanted to have some other mode of transportation than walking or taxis. She had done some research online, so she had some ideas of what she might want to buy. She would go out to look after church on Sunday, she decided. It always seemed to help her follow through if she made a plan.

On Sunday, she "hit a triple," as she put it later to Marty. She went to the early church service that day and then to adult Bible study. There were about a dozen or so people gathered together in the library of the small Lutheran church.

"Welcome, welcome," said a perky and very petite woman named Nancy. "Please have a seat and tell us who you are and how you came to us today."

Jillian briefly explained to the group about her recent move and that she had been coming to church there for a few weeks now, but had gone to the late service. She actually had met one woman at the table, Sheila, the week prior, and she also noticed a familiar-looking man she had seen at the late service one of the Sundays. He was the type one didn't easily forget, one who stood out in a crowd. At six-foot-three, with curly light brown hair, an athletic build, and deep blue eyes, he no doubt caught a good number of female eyes. Jillian surmised that he was in his early forties, if even that. The members of the group introduced themselves one by one, and she found out that the man's name was Drew Alexander. He was an accountant, he said during introductions, and later she found out he worked in his family's own firm.

Nancy, the woman who had welcomed her, was a widow with six grown children. She was a delightful person and was leading the study that day. The story was about Joseph and his brothers, and the theme was betrayal. The group discussed how difficult it must have been for Joseph to suffer betrayal at the hands of people he loved and trusted. As usual, Jillian thought God had impeccable timing, as she had just been reprocessing some of her past heartache and betrayal while watching O.R.

Nancy shared some of the feelings she had experienced when her husband had died. He had been only thirty-six years old when he was diagnosed with pancreatic cancer. He was a good husband, father, and a devout church member. Everyone had prayed for Ed to get better, but he died nonetheless. At the time, Nancy had felt betrayed in a way—by God. Jillian understood that feeling. It had sometimes happened to her, especially in her younger years. But as time passed, and as she matured in years and in her faith, she realized that God had been with her throughout it all. She figured out that God has a way of making good come out of bad situations. Her daughter was prime proof of that. Nancy had shared similar sentiments, and Jillian knew that this woman would become a friend of hers sometime soon.

After the Bible study, there was just enough time to catch a cup of coffee before the second service began. Drew came over to Jillian as she put a touch of cream into her steaming cup.

"How are you enjoying Southern California, Jillian?" he asked.

"I like it—a lot. Especially right now, in winter. I cannot seriously say that I miss snow, ice, and below-freezing temperatures."

"I can't say that I've ever experienced below-freezing temperatures, and sincerely hope that I never do," he said.

Jillian laughed. "I love that I am going to buy a bike today and can actually ride it."

"What kind are you buying?"

"I'm thinking of a cyclocross. Or maybe just a road bike. I did some research online and have a short list of favorites. Do you ride?"

"I used to. I could help you look for one—that is, if you wanted me to."

The way he said it made her feel like he would be hurt if she said no. Besides, she had given herself permission to date again, even if this might not qualify as a date.

"Sure, but you would have to do the driving. I don't have a car out here, at least not yet. That is part of the reason I am getting a bike."

"No problem. We could go now if you would like, and maybe we could catch some lunch afterward."

"Sounds like a plan," Jillian said. *And now it sounds like we are in the date category.*

Jillian and Drew checked out three different bicycle shops and at least a dozen bikes before Jillian decided to support a company from her home state with the purchase of a Trek cyclocross, manufactured not far from where she had lived for the past ten years.

Drew took a photo on Jillian's smartphone of her straddling her new, bright-colored bike. With all the cars in Los Angeles, she wanted to make certain to stand out on the streets. She sent the photo to Marty. A helmet, water bottle, and a good lock rounded out her acquisitions for the day. She walked her new prized possession out the front door of the shop to Drew's vehicle. After taking off the front tire, Drew loaded the bike and her equipment into the back of his new Mercedes SUV.

Drew drove them to the ocean, where he treated her to lunch at an upscale cafe. She could tell that Drew was accustomed to nice things. Earlier he had suggested that she buy a bike that cost more than $4,000, but she ended up with one that was a little less than half that price, not ready to commit so much money to anything until she knew she would really use it the way she hoped to. Even then, she wasn't sure she would ever need a $4,000 bicycle for any reason.

Drew ordered scallops, and Jillian ordered a small grilled salmon salad, which was delicious. They had a table with a fantastic view of the ocean. The weather was fabulous, and Jillian hoped it would still be that way when she got home. Even though she was enjoying their outing, she couldn't wait to get home to try out her new bike before it got dark.

While they polished off their lunches, they talked about their families. Drew came from a long line of accountants and was in a partnership with his father and uncle. He had one sister who lived in San Diego and who was married to an attorney. His mother had never worked outside of the home, but was active in charitable work and rose gardening.

Jillian told him about her nursing degrees. He seemed impressed by this, and she told him about Marty being a student at Harvard Medical School and her current internship in Senegal.

"How could you let your daughter go to a place like that?"

The question took her by surprise. She told him that she and Marty had lived in Africa for eight years and that Marty had known what she wanted to do with her life since she was a ten-year-old.

"We were visiting some of my young patients in the hospital

when she told me, 'I want to help children not go blind or get sick from dirty water. Someday I'm going to find a cure, Mom.' How do you argue with that?"

Drew said, "I guess you can't," but Jillian could tell he didn't really understand or approve, and he politely changed the subject.

"Do you like concerts?" he asked her.

"Yes, I enjoy all kinds of music," she answered truthfully. She had everything from country to jazz, opera to hip hop, show tunes to Christian, classical to classic rock on her computer playlist.

"The Philharmonic is doing Mahler's 6th next Saturday. Would you care to join me?"

"Yes, that sounds wonderful," Jillian said, surprising herself with her quick response. She did enjoy "the symphony," and had even taken an elective class by that very name as an undergraduate at UW. And she also reminded herself that she had made dating one of her goals when she began this adventure. This seemed to be another step in the right direction.

They talked about the logistics for the evening at the Philharmonic, and then Jillian remembered to ask him if he knew of any book clubs in their area. He said it was her lucky day, as he was in one and she would be very welcome to join. They were going to meet a week from Wednesday, in fact. Jillian felt like it was indeed a lucky day, and smiled as they headed for the SUV.

Drew drove her home in time to try out her bike before it got dark. She told him her address and explained her living situation and current position, and how she had taken it so she could devote her time to writing. He looked surprised, and just as he had with the discussion of Marty's work, he didn't seem to understand or approve of her situation. As the conversation progressed, she got the impression that he thought of her current endeavor as a "passing phase," one he hoped she would get over—soon.

They turned into the circle drive to Mr. Romano's house.

"Thank you for everything, Drew—the shopping, the lunch,

the conversation, the lugging," she said, adding that last part as they pulled her new investment out of the vehicle in the driveway.

"Thank you for joining me. I usually have dinner at my parents' house and then play golf with my dad. This was a nice change."

Jillian found it a bit unusual that Drew had such a routine, but also thought it was nice that he was close to his family, especially since he was fairly recently single. Drew had told her that he had been divorced two years before. He hadn't gone into detail, but it sounded like his ex-wife had been the one to call it off. Jillian wondered why.

Just looking at Drew, Jillian had difficulty believing that he was still available after two years. He had good looks, money, a fancy car, and a steady job—one that he would most likely have for life. Many women would love a list of attributes like that in a man. *Too bad I'm not one of them,* she thought to herself. She scolded herself inwardly for thinking such a thought when she had just met Drew. She made a conscious decision to give him a real chance. There had been enough times in her life when she had greatly misjudged people by not allowing enough time to find out who the person really was. She owed Drew, and herself, more than that.

She smiled as they exchanged phone numbers, then said goodbye. He drove slowly down the driveway. He had offered to help take the bike back to her cottage, but she was pretty certain that would be a huge mistake and might even be cause for dismissal. She told him she was going out to ride this bike in just a few minutes, as soon as she threw on some different clothes. Reluctantly, he had agreed.

Jillian took her bike and equipment through the gate. She left the bike and helmet just inside, and practically ran to the cottage. When she got to the back of the garage, she stopped short to make certain she was not interrupting Mr. Romano, who might be outside on this beautiful afternoon. She knew that if it were her house and her pool, she would be in it. She peered around the corner. The coast was clear, so she scampered to her place, changed, and headed out for her inaugural ride.

She glided down the driveway and out onto the boulevard. Jillian loved the way things always seemed different when riding bike. She noticed things in the neighborhood that she had never seen before—a statue in the corner of a yard, a swing set in a back yard, different types of flowers and shrubs, and a beautiful red convertible in someone's open garage. She returned to the house an hour later, happy, excited, and a tad winded.

She had made a good choice. The bicycle had been one of those she had on her list, and it had high ratings on the Internet. It rode like a dream on the street, but she could tell she could also take it on a trail, should she be able to find one. Checking for bike trails and routes in the area would be her next Internet search project.

Jillian rode up the driveway and hopped off in front of the iron gate. She successfully turned the key, which she stored in a small pouch she bought just for it and her phone, and took her new prized possession back to the cottage. The weather was clear, so she left it out on her little patio, as close to the cottage as she could. She guessed she would have to bring it in when it rained, as she didn't really have any other options.

After making a sandwich and enjoying a hot shower, she posted in her blog. She decided to talk about "first impressions." She wanted to hear from people about first impressions they had of people, especially in the dating area. She shared, without going into major detail, how she had once been "so wrong" about someone she thought had been "so right"—twice, in fact. The post generated some thoughtful responses.

One person wrote about how her sister had absolutely abhorred a man at work. The woman had even thought about leaving her employment because she couldn't stand him. She ended up being assigned to a special project with him and learned what sort of person he really was. They ended up married within the year, had been together now for ten years, and had two young children.

Another person posted about how he kept searching and searching for the right person to marry, when it occurred to him that a woman who had been his good friend since junior high had been right there all along. It took him a while, but he finally figured out that she was the best person in his life. They had married three years ago. Unfortunately, she had recently died in an accident. That was what had drawn him to the blog for broken hearts. His only regret in the relationship was that he had wasted so much time figuring things out, but he was grateful for the time they had had as both friends and as spouses. Others responded with words of encouragement to this gentleman, as did Jillian. Again, she felt that this blog was a real gift.

When Jillian went to bed that night, she had a feeling she was on the right path. She said her prayers, thanking God for her employment, her little cottage, a church with a good pastor and a Bible study, her new bike, new friends, and a date to top it off. Not bad. Not bad at all. She ended her litany as she usually did, praying for her daughter—her happiness, her safety and her work—and as had become somewhat of a habit at this point, praying for Mr. Romano, that God would give him whatever God saw that he needed.

❖

The next morning, it was back to work. Jillian happily strode into the kitchen on a sunny morning, thinking that if it stayed nice outside that afternoon, she could go for a ride after she was done cleaning. She could tell her muscles were a little sore, and she wanted to keep them loosened up. A riding routine was what she needed to get into better physical shape. She had always kept herself trim and toned, and she wasn't about to start letting that slip now.

Jillian stopped short when her eyes spied a note on the counter. There had been no more notes since she had left that one rather rude message for Mr. Romano weeks before. She had regretted writing it many times over since that day. She had written it in frustration and anger, which was never a good idea. She was afraid to look, but of course, she had to read it. She tentatively picked it up and read:

You may store your bicycle in the garage if you wish.

Jillian could hardly believe it. Mr. Romano must have seen her riding, or more likely, noticed the bike's arrival when she and Drew had driven up to unload it. If so, she was so happy she had not let Drew come through the gate with her. She didn't know the protocol on visitors yet. That was another item to check on with Mr. Mack, as her employment "book" failed to address the issue.

She looked at the note again to make sure she had read it correctly. She had. Perhaps it was because Mr. Romano was a bike rider himself—or had been at one time at least. That assumption was based on a very nice bike hanging on hooks from the garage ceiling, although she had never seen it down or used since her arrival. No matter what his reason was for the offer, she was very pleasantly surprised. Her blog post about first impressions flashed through her mind briefly. She wrote a simple note back and left it next to the other one.

Thank you so much.

The unexpected note made for a most pleasant Monday, and the time flew by. Fortunately, the afternoon weather was still nice as Jillian ended her workday, and she would get to ride her new bike in just a few short minutes. As she finished her work in the kitchen, she felt optimistic and like the world was full of possibilities. For her—for *everyone,* she thought, as she looked at the two

Kathy J. Jacobson

notes on the counter one last time before leaving the house for the day.

Jillian took another hour-long bike ride, exploring a different part of the neighborhood than she had the day before. Bike riding was a great way to get a feel for an area. On this ride, she found more Storybook style homes, some Spanish mission designs, along with some very modern creations. She enjoyed the architecture of the area, which varied greatly from the architecture in her home region.

Jillian met a woman while on her ride, a young mother named Meredith who was out pushing a stroller. The woman seemed startled when Jillian halted her bike and began talking to her. After Meredith realized Jillian meant her no harm, she introduced herself, and they talked for a few minutes. Her baby's name was Charles, but she liked to call him Charlie. As Jillian rode away from Meredith and Charlie, she had to remind herself that she was not in the Midwest anymore. People didn't just stop strangers on the street and begin a conversation in other parts of the country as often as they tended to where she hailed from.

Jillian felt ravenous when she returned home. She decided that she had better start making some meals ahead of time so she could just heat them up when she got back from her rides. The riding was going to change her daily routine, she could tell, and in a good way. Again, as she had in the morning, she felt very optimistic about pretty much everything, and it was reflected in her blog entry that night. Her post was about how good it felt to turn personal goals into realities. She also wrote about "possibilities."

Chapter Seven

On Saturday morning of that week, Mr. Mack called her. Her heart was pounding when she saw his number flash on her cell. *This is it. I'm getting fired.*

"Ms. Johnson?" he asked, almost like he was surprised to hear her answer. He continued, "Is everything all right?"

"I was just about to ask you the same thing, Mr. Mack," Jillian responded.

"I just hadn't heard from you, or Mr. Romano, in six weeks. I wanted to make certain that you...that everything was okay."

"Everything is fine, at least to my knowledge."

"That's wonderful to hear." He paused. "Congratulations. You've lasted longer in this position than anyone else has in the past two years."

Six weeks is the record? Jillian found that difficult to believe.

"Thank you," she answered, still amazed by the statistic.

"Well, I will let you go. Please don't hesitate to call if there are any issues."

"I won't. Thank you for checking on me."

She had to laugh at his serious concern for her well-being, but then decided it was nice to have someone check up on her, especially since most of her friends were thousands of miles away, Marty was in Senegal, and her new friends were not what she would consider close yet.

Jillian pondered the fact that she had a record-setting employment record at the six-week mark. She decided she would celebrate by baking something special this week. She had purchased some small heart-shaped tins at the store, as Valentine's Day was the next Friday. She had given her tins away when she moved. Each year at Valentine's Day, she and Marty made their favorite dark chocolate and raspberry torte recipe in those four small tins. It had taken some time playing around with the recipe to get it to work just right in the special tins, but the result was worth it.

They had each decorated two of them, trying to outdo one another with their designs. Marty almost always "won," as she was more naturally artistic, but Jillian had learned a few things from watching her daughter over the years. She would make the recipe and decorate them in Marty's honor. Maybe she could give one to Drew. She felt like she was getting ahead of herself, though, and thought she should wait and see how the big date at the symphony went that evening before she made any additional plans.

Jillian had taken a taxi the day before to go shopping for a dress, shoes, and a clutch for the evening out. She hated to miss her bike ride, but it had been a bit of a dreary day, so it made missing it a bit easier. She found a simple but elegant black dress. The woman in the shop had tried to talk her into something much more expensive and ornate, but if she had purchased the other dress, Jillian wasn't sure where or when she would ever wear it again. Some women didn't worry about things like that. Some women never wore a dress more than once. But Jillian was definitely not one of those women.

Again, she thought of her friends in Tanzania, some with only one pair of pants and two shirts—one for the week, one for Sunday, or one dress for the week and another for church. And shoes—if you had them at all—were repaired over and over until they could no longer be fixed. She wondered what they would think about people wearing an article of clothing only once.

She headed home, feeling fortunate to find something that she actually liked, that she could wear again, and wasn't *too* expensive. Everything was a bit more expensive than what she was used to, but she had been prepared for that to be the case in the larger city.

Drew picked her up at seven p.m. sharp. She met him at the top of the driveway near the gate to the back yard. He was dressed in a dark suit that she was sure cost more than her new bicycle, looking even more handsome than he had on Sunday. He opened the car door for her from inside the vehicle, which didn't particularly impress her, and she slid in. Perhaps he thought she might not like the more old-fashioned courtesies, but she always appreciated them, especially early on in relationships.

They drove into the city and parked in a reserved space in the garage under the performance venue. At 7:40 p.m., they walked into the stunning Walt Disney Concert Hall and were seated in the front orchestra section. She was impressed, until Drew mentioned as they sat down that the firm had season tickets. She guessed they were sitting in them that evening and that the car was parked in the firm's reserved parking space as well. She didn't mind, however. It was just wonderful to be in this special place, about to listen to an outstanding orchestra.

Jillian had forgotten how intoxicating live classical music could be. She was in a trance when the strings played, only interrupted from time to time by the brass and percussion. It was an enchanting program. Drew, however, seemed as though he couldn't have cared less about the music. It appeared to Jillian that he was there to meet and greet people. It was an important place to be seen by his clients, no doubt.

Jillian tried to discuss some of her thoughts about the music at intermission, but eventually gave up as Drew was clearly not interested. Instead, she felt like she was "the girl on his arm" for the evening, whether or not that was really the case. He introduced her to many people as a nurse who recently relocated to the area from the Midwest. Jillian wondered what his clients and associates would think if they knew what she currently did for a living, where she resided, and what her new career plans were.

After the concert, they walked next door to a brasserie for dessert and coffee. It was a classy atmosphere, and the place was filled with after-concert goers. By the time they left, the director of the orchestra and his personal entourage had arrived at a reserved table. Again, Drew seemed to know many of the people and introduced Jillian in the same manner as he had earlier in the evening to each of them. She had been tempted several times to give them the real story, but she didn't want to ruin the evening for Drew, or herself.

While they were sipping their hot drinks, Drew filled her in on who some of the people were, who they worked for, or what company they owned. Their names and their firms meant nothing to Jillian, but it was clear that they did to Drew.

They made small talk over dessert, and Drew made a plan to pick Jillian up for the book club on Wednesday evening. All of a sudden, Jillian's social calendar was exploding—at least compared to it being a complete zero during her first month living in L.A.

They were quiet as they drove home. Unfortunately, at least for Jillian, it was not a comfortable quiet, but that was okay. That was usual, she told herself, when people were on first or second dates and didn't know each other very well yet.

When they arrived at her house, Drew stopped the vehicle near the gate. He took her hand and squeezed it, and said goodnight. She said goodnight and quickly climbed out of the vehicle. He may have been a bit surprised by her quick departure, but she wasn't ready for any kind of big goodnight scene. Not yet.

Drew had waited to make sure she got through the gate to the back yard, which she appreciated. She was happy that she had remembered that she needed to punch a code into a pad on the garage so that the alarm system didn't sound. It actually unlocked the gate automatically for her, so it was nice not to have to fumble with the key in the semi-darkness. Too bad she couldn't use that all the time, but it was only set to work after ten p.m. each evening. She turned back to Drew, smiled, and waved as she headed through the gate.

It was fairly well-lit on the side of the garage, but she used her cell phone flashlight anyway since maneuvering on cobblestone could be tricky at night. Jillian realized how tired she was as she started back through the yard. It was after midnight, and the next morning was church. She wanted to go to Bible study, too.

Jillian stepped out of her shoes as she walked through the grassy part of the yard, amazed that she could do such a thing in February. She had to get out of these new heels. Her feet hurt, but considering they were new shoes, it could have been much worse. She had once wore an ill-advised pair of shoes walking about New York City and could barely walk the next day. The shoes had caused blisters, and her feet were swollen. It had been a very foolish move to put fashion above common sense on that occasion.

Once inside the cottage, she hung up her dress, peeled off her nylons, and put on her favorite flannel pants and long-sleeved V-neck sleep shirt. *That's more like it.*

After washing her face, brushing her teeth, and setting her alarm, Jillian hopped into bed and thought about the evening. She had enjoyed the concert tremendously. The rest of the evening—it was just not her. It was fun. It was interesting. She was game for almost anything, but she knew she couldn't take a steady diet of that kind of life. She wondered for a moment if that was the reason

Drew wasn't married any longer. Maybe his ex-wife couldn't take a steady diet of that kind of life either. She wondered this only for another minute, as she quickly fell into a deep sleep.

❖

Drew was not at church the next morning. Jillian's first thought was that he was angry about her quick and rather evasive exit out of his vehicle the night before, but he called later in the day to apologize for not making it. He said something had come up with work, and he had to attend to it. He asked her if she was free, but Jillian just wanted to take a bike ride and then relax. She made the excuse that she and Marty had a video chat scheduled, which was true enough, and that she had some other things she really needed to get done before work the next day—*like post in her blog*—but she didn't tell him this, as he did not seem very interested in her writing the last time she had mentioned it.

After a bike ride, a short rest, and a load of laundry, her cell phone chirped to notify her it was time to go online for the video call.

"Hi Mom," Marty said. She was sitting in a medical office this time rather than her apartment.

"I see you are at work early," Jillian remarked.

"Actually, I've been here all night. We had a couple emergencies. You know how that goes."

Her usually perky daughter looked exhausted. Even though Marty was there for research and teaching, the interns also worked as emergency staff at the hospitals and clinics because well-trained medical personnel was scarce.

"Will you get to go home any time soon?" Jillian asked.

"Probably not, but as soon as we are done talking, I'm going to lie down on the cot in the back room."

"I won't be long-winded then," Jillian said.

Jillian knew what it felt like to be up all night and then have to keep working. You had to get your rest when you could through-out the day—for your sake and for your patients' sakes. Most mis-takes that were made by medical personnel were made by tired, overworked nurses and doctors.

Jillian filled her in about her week, beginning with the new bike, the lunch out, the symphony, and dessert at the brasserie.

"Well, that was quite a week. I'm so happy you got your bike, Mom. And the night at the symphony sounds fantastic, especially the music."

They were so much alike, it was amazing to Jillian.

"This guy, Drew—is he handsome?" Marty asked in a matter-of-fact way.

"Yes. Very."

"Has a lot of money?"

"Ditto."

"Drives a fancy car, too, I suppose?"

Jillian nodded.

"What does he do for a living?"

"He's an accountant. Family firm. Long line of them."

"You're not very interested, are you?" The girl sure knew her mother.

"Not at this point in time. I suppose I should be, but I'm not sure he's my type. And I'm not sure that I'm his either. I'll give him some more chances, though. And if nothing else, I think we could be friends. Wednesday night, he is taking me to his book club, so I think I may get to see a different side of him in that setting. It is nice that he goes to church, although I wonder a bit about his motives."

"What do you mean?"

Jillian told Marty how Drew had seemed at the concert and res-taurant—like he was there to "see and be seen." Jillian wondered if church fell into that same category and sincerely hoped that was not the case.

They talked a bit about Marty's week, especially about the emergencies she had handled during the night. Jillian was proud of Marty and knew that she was an excellent doctor. Then Jillian told her daughter to go to sleep, hoping that Marty could get a power-nap in before the next case, if nothing else.

"Lala salama. Love you, honey," Jillian said.

"Lala salama. Love you, too, Mama!" Their video call disconnected, but Jillian's laptop remained open.

Jillian decided to look up the recipe for her dark chocolate-raspberry torte in her documents file and checked to see what she needed from the store. She would make the tortes on Thursday evening. She was only missing two small ingredients, so she would be able to take her bike to the store to get them. It had only been one week since she got the new bike, and she could already feel the difference in her muscle-tone and energy level.

Later that evening, she blogged about the benefits of exercise in dealing with stress, including loss, grief, and general heartbreak. It was a wonderful way to improve one's health, to get more energy and lift one's spirits. It released endorphins that actually improved one's mood. Yes, this bike had been a good choice. Her other choices of the week—they were still up for debate.

❖

On Wednesday night, Drew picked Jillian up around 6:30 p.m., and they headed a few miles away to the home of a woman named Karen Wilson. Karen was about Jillian's age or slightly older, married to a man name Robert, an attorney who was always working and never home, according to Karen. That was the reason she volunteered to host the book club at her house every month. That, and she loved to cook and entertain.

The book the club had just read was *Cutting for Stone*. Jillian had not just *read* it, but had read it twice. Even though it had been a few years, it had been a special book to her as it was set in Africa, in the country of Ethiopia. She had been to Addis Ababa once. The book club members, with the exception of Karen, had looked at her like she was from Mars when she talked about Africa. She noticed Drew, who looked bored at hearing her story once again.

Jillian shared her insights on the book and talked about the realities of practicing medicine in such a place. She also told them about Marty and her current work. For a moment, she thought that they didn't believe her. She was relieved when it was time to move on to another person.

Two other people spoke about their reactions to the book. Then it was time to receive the title of the next one. Their next read would be *The Brief Wondrous Life of Oscar Wao*.

An anemic-looking woman named Sandra asked, "Why do we have to keep reading all these *foreign* books?"

"We need to keep expanding our knowledge, Sandra. Not all of us are as fortunate as Jillian, who has lived and worked in another culture," Karen replied. Jillian smiled at her, appreciating Karen's affirmation of her past experiences.

Jillian hoped they had the book at the library. Most of the members were buying their copies and gave her the name of their favored bookstore.

After the discussion, they had some healthy snacks. As much as she enjoyed cookies, brownies, and cheese and crackers—typical Midwestern book club fare—Jillian was impressed and happy to have a selection of wiser choices. Karen served Caprese salad, cucumber cups filled with spicy crab, grilled asparagus spears, pita bread with hummus, fresh fruits, and smoked fish with a delightful sauce of Karen's own creation. Jillian could see why Karen liked to entertain. She clearly had a flare for cooking, and the presentation of the array of foods looked professionally done.

Karen came up to her as they mingled about the large, open living/dining area. She told Jillian how much she appreciated her perspective on the book and how wonderful it was to have someone in the group who had such unique experiences. Jillian could tell that she meant it, and Jillian felt that she and Karen had serious potential in the friend category. They exchanged phone numbers on their cells. Jillian thought that Karen seemed lonely. There was a lot of that going around the area, she thought.

Drew seemed completely bored by the evening. In fact, based on his comments, of which there were very few, Jillian was pretty sure that he had never even read the book, or if he had, only a portion of it. The only time he seemed "interested" was during the social time after the club meeting. Jillian got the same feeling again that she had after the Philharmonic and restaurant outings—that Drew was there to be seen. It was as if his entire life was a wise business move. She suspected that some of the people in his club were his firm's clientele.

Few of the women in the club worked outside of the home, and many seemed to have little to talk about during refreshments other than what they had purchased since their last meeting. The few other men who attended stood with Drew and talked about business and then golf. Jillian overheard them make plans to play together on Saturday morning.

Drew took her home after the refreshments, as he had an early meeting the next morning. He apologized for not going out afterward, but Jillian was fine with that, as her day would start fairly early as well. This time they stopped in her driveway, he jumped out of the car as soon as he put it into park. She did as well. He met her on the other side of the vehicle, the motor still running.

"What are you doing Friday night?" he asked.

"No plans at the moment. You?"

"I was thinking it would be nice to go to dinner," he said, inching closer to her.

"Yes, that would be nice," she said, backing up slightly.

He must have noticed, so he didn't push it. He was smart enough not to be too aggressive, at least.

They said goodnight, and he hopped back into the SUV, driving very slowly down the driveway again, almost like he was hoping she would stop him and invite him in. As she headed through the yard to the cottage, she felt excited. She had liked Karen and, for the most part, had enjoyed the discussion of the book. She was excited to be reading again and couldn't wait to get her new book. Tomorrow evening, she would take a taxi to the library.

❖

The next night, after a successful library run, Jillian made her Valentine tortes. They turned out very well, and she sent a photo of them to Marty on her phone. She would keep one torte for herself, give one to Drew the next evening, and one to Nancy at church Sunday morning, but wondered what to do with the other. She thought of Mr. Romano, but after the pilau dish incident, she wasn't certain that it would be a good idea. She had a little war going on in her head while making the decision. She had bought some cute Valentine paper plates, so she could use those for all the tortes. She finally decided that if Mr. Romano threw it out, he threw it out, and she wrapped the three to give away.

At the end of the day, which was also the end of her work week, she put the torte into Mr. Romano's refrigerator. It looked almost professionally baked. She decided she had best leave a note.

There is a little something in the fridge for you.
If you don't care for the dessert, feel free to throw it away.

She went back to her cottage and got ready for the evening. As she showered and dressed, she wished that she were more excited about this dinner out. It was Valentine's Day, for goodness sake! She should be thrilled to be going to dinner with a handsome man. Instead, she was beginning to feel like she was just going through the motions, and that didn't seem very fair to her date.

She would have to reevaluate the situation after the evening. She didn't want to lead Drew on. She knew how that felt—big time.

They drove to Topanga Canyon, to a waterfront fish and seafood restaurant along the Pacific Coast Highway. There, Jillian had the best ocean fish she had ever tasted. The place was ridiculously busy with all the couples there to celebrate Valentine's Day, and it had been difficult to hear each other talk at times. In some ways, she wished she had just offered to make dinner for Drew at his place. They could have had the tortes for dessert. But it was too late now. And perhaps that would not have been a wise suggestion considering the way she felt—or didn't feel.

Jillian looked around the crowded venue and watched the people. She wondered which couples were truly in love and which were not. Valentine's Day had never been one of Jillian's favorite holidays. It always seemed to separate people—the ones who had someone special to love them, whom they loved, and the ones who didn't. Somewhere between the swordfish and the creme brûlée, she realized she was still in the latter category.

Drew was a nice guy. She wouldn't mind doing things with him as a friend, but she was pretty sure that she could never really love this man. All he did was talk about money, name-drop, or go on and on about his golf game. Jillian liked golf, but was not obsessed with it like he obviously was. The other main topic of discussion was whatever he, or someone he knew, had just purchased, or were planning to buy. She just didn't understand this world, she guessed. How much money one spent, and how many things one bought, did not impress her, as it obviously impressed Drew.

They were quiet again on the ride home, and again, not the comfortable kind of silence. Jillian wished they had not gone so far away from home for dinner so that the ride could have been shorter. She felt guilty for thinking that way, but she couldn't help it.

Once they got to her driveway, Drew again hopped out of the vehicle. This time he was quicker and met her at the door of the SUV. As soon as she stood up, he grabbed her and kissed her. It surprised her so much that she almost felt like slapping him. Not a good sign for their relationship, she thought to herself as she quickly ended the kiss and pulled away as politely as she could.

She told him not to forget his chocolate torte in the back seat. He said he wouldn't and thanked her. Before he could do something like kiss her again, she turned to the pad on the garage and punched in the code. The door clicked open, and she grabbed for it.

"Goodnight, Drew. Thank you for dinner. It was a lovely place and wonderful food," Jillian said sincerely. That was the best she could do, considering she was not feeling very comfortable about the Drew situation at that particular moment. She was glad that the next day was Saturday and not Sunday. At least she had a day before she had to see him again, as he was busy with the golf outing. Again, it was not a very good sign to be feeling that way about one's date.

Once at the cottage, she undressed and thought about the last couple of days. The book club was fun, and she liked Karen. Jillian made a mental note to give her a call sometime very soon. She had found a copy of their next book club book at the library and had started reading it. She was enjoying it so far, but hadn't had enough time to delve very deeply into it. Maybe the following day she could do some serious damage. Once Jillian got into a book, it was hard for her to put it down.

Thinking about reading made her think about all the books in the main house. One thing that had struck her while cleaning over the past weeks was the fact that there were no newer titles in that beautiful library—not one.

She wondered if Mr. Romano had given up on reading new books, along with the other things he seemed to have given up on.

She also wondered how he had spent his evening. And lastly, she hoped he hadn't thrown away the chocolate torte.

❖

Sunday came, and Jillian saw Drew at Bible study. He had gone to the early church service, since he wanted to go golfing with his dad, uncle, and a new client later in the day. She walked out to this vehicle with him as there was still some time before the late service began.

"How did you like the torte?" Jillian asked, as they walked toward the Mercedes.

"It was wonderful. Thank you."

"It's a recipe Marty and I enjoyed making every Valentine's Day. The decorating was our favorite part, though."

He smiled. "Yes, I can imagine." He looked at his watch. It was clear he was in a hurry to get going.

"Have a good game, and week," she said to him.

"You, too. I'll give you a call when I'm done with golf," he said, winking and starting the engine. He started to pull away, and she happened to glance into his vehicle. There on the back seat sat the plate with the chocolate torte, still wrapped. He had never even taken it into his house, let alone try it. Perhaps she wasn't such a bad judge of character after all. She had thought Drew was a bit of a fake before. Now she knew that he was.

She finished *The Brief Wondrous Life of Oscar Wao* later that day. Once she had time to sit down and read it, she couldn't stop. Later she realized that Drew had never called as she said he would, but that was fine with her and confirmed once again in her mind that he was not a completely honest person. She hoped he was more honest in his business dealings than he was in his personal ones.

❖

On Monday morning, she ran to the main house in the rain. Karen Carpenter's song rang in her ears: *"Rainy days and Mondays always get me down."* Actually, Jillian didn't feel down. She had been writing, biking, baking, out on a couple of dates, had gone to a book club, and had already finished the next book. The only thing getting her down was the good possibility that she wouldn't be bike riding that day due to the weather.

When Jillian entered the kitchen, she just *had* to look. She slowly opened the refrigerator to see if the torte was still in there. It was not. She could barely get herself to peek, but she slowly opened the kitchen trash bin. It wasn't there either. She took the almost full bag to the garage and was happy that she didn't see the heart-shaped torte in the garbage there either. It was funny how such a little discovery seemed to "make her day."

When she came back to the house after lunch, she brought the library book with her, holding it under her rain jacket. She thought she would leave it for Mr. Romano to read. It wasn't due back to the library for two weeks. She bet he could read it just as quickly as she had, maybe even faster, with all the reading he had done. At the end of the day, she left a note next to the book.

Thought you might like to read this.

She walked back to cottage. It was no longer raining, so she decided to take a walk around the neighborhood. She didn't want to get her bike all messy and didn't care to ride on the slick streets after a day of rain. A walk would have to suffice.

❖

There were two subjects in her blog post that evening. The first was about honesty. The second was about disappointments. She had Drew and some of his behaviors over the past week in mind as she wrote. Most people responded that honesty, even if it sometimes hurt, was better than dishonesty in any form, and that dishonesty was a leading cause of disappointments in relationships.

Indeed, there was truth to that. Jillian hadn't appreciated that Drew had been less than completely honest with her, and it disappointed her. And then she realized that she was no better. She knew she needed to be more honest with him in the future. For instance, it might be a good idea to let him know how she felt—that they could be friends of some sort but definitely nothing more.

Chapter Eight

The library book sat in the same exact spot Jillian had left it for the next few days, but the note was gone. *Oh well, if he doesn't want to read it, no big deal.* She decided to leave it on the counter until was time to take it back to the library. Maybe he was reading something else right now, she thought. There was always a book on the table in the library, next to the reading glasses. Maybe he doesn't like reading two books at once. Many people don't care to do that.

That night, however, Jillian made a discovery by accident. The moonlight was pouring into her cottage window, as she hadn't shut the blinds all the way. She went to the window to pull the blinds and instinctively peered out.

She noticed a light shining on the rose bushes, coming from the kitchen. Her first thought was that Mr. Romano was ill. Her parents had left a light on in their farmhouse one night by mistake. The next morning, two neighbors called to make sure that everything was okay. Jillian hoped everything was okay with Mr. Romano.

Jillian looked more closely. Although it was a bit of a distance, she was quite certain that Mr. Romano was sitting at the counter reading the book, his reading glasses sitting at the end of his nose.

She wondered if he had just started reading it or if he had been doing that each night. She went back to bed, but had trouble falling back to sleep. She kept thinking of him reading so secretively, not wanting her, or anyone, to know what was going on in his life. She closed her eyes again, not to sleep, but to say another prayer for him.

The next morning, the book was in the exact spot that she had left it the first day, looking completely untouched. *Pretty sneaky*, she thought, and she wondered if he would be back reading again that night, and thought if she wasn't too tired, she might wait to see.

Jillian was a bit disappointed later that night. If any reading occurred, it was much later than she was willing to stay up. Maybe he had finished the book already, but she decided to leave it on the counter until she had to return it, just in case.

There was no sign of him reading the next night. She decided that she was being ridiculous, so that was the last night she stayed up. She took the book back to the library and got another one she thought he would like, *The Fortunate Flowers*. She put it on the counter, with the same note as before.

She wasn't going to do it, but she couldn't seem to help herself. She found herself peering out the window that night, and there he was again, reading away. Next time, she would get more than one book. The man was a voracious reader, and once he got a taste for some of these newer titles, she knew he would want to read even more.

Over the next month, she guessed that he had read at least a dozen books. He always left them sitting on the counter looking completely undisturbed. Jillian could live with that, but someday, she would ask him what he thought about one of them, even if it meant she knew he was reading them.

In the meantime, Jillian and Karen from the book club had gotten together a few times for lunch on the weekends, since Robert worked even then.

"I don't know what to do about it, Jillian," Karen said. "The man works *all* the time. I once worried that he was having an affair, but I have sources I trust that tell me that he really *is* working."

Jillian thought back to her dad. He was a great man, and so hard-working, but sometimes too hard-working.

Jillian told her, "My mom used to get disgusted with my dad sometimes. He worked five full days and Saturday morning at the machine shop, then came home and farmed the rest of the evenings and most of the weekend. Every once in a while, she would just tell him, 'Martin, Jillian and I are going to a movie, or a dinner, or whatever—with, or without, you.' We would be all set to go, so he would know that we meant business. She would never do it if it was harvest season, but if it was just a regular Saturday night or Sunday afternoon, she just put her foot down. Usually, he would say, 'Give me a few minutes to wash up and change,' and then we were all on our way." Jillian could see the cogs moving in Karen's brain as she relayed that story.

On another occasion, Jillian had suggested that they go for a walk around Karen's neighborhood. Karen had mentioned that she was beginning to get stiff every morning when she got up, and she was only a couple of years older than Jillian.

Jillian had asked, "What do you do for exercise, Karen?"

"What exercise?" had been her response.

Jillian suggested a walking plan that she had once used with members of the church where she had been a parish nurse. Of all her nursing positions, parish nursing had been her favorite, with the exception of the pay. There was so much variety. She loved visiting the shut-in elderly and disabled members, taking their blood pressures, checking to make sure they were taking their medications, eating right, and had food in their refrigerators, and just talking with lonely souls.

She had also led a "healthy living group" for church members who wanted to improve their health, which grew to be so huge that she had to break it into two separate groups.

Jillian also had the opportunity to work with the homeless. Even when she and Marty moved to Madison, they had helped with meals for the homeless and indigent a number of times per year, and always on Christmas Day.

Thinking about her parish nurse days suddenly conjured up another ghost from the past, and the second big disappointment of her life in the romance area. Perhaps it was even worst than the first, considering she was more mature and should have been able, she thought later, to have seen through this person's guise.

Jillian and Marty had landed in the city of Milwaukee upon their return to the States. Jillian had accepted the call to be the parish nurse at a large downtown church. The first year, with all the different ministry and nursing tasks, had been fun and fulfilling. She had made many friends in the community, and the work didn't even seem like work.

At the beginning of her second year, Pastor Scott Bradford happened. He was just a year older than Jillian. He was joining the staff as a pastor, having been a well-loved solo pastor at his previous church in Iowa, where he had served for ten years. His wife had died of cancer three years before, and he had felt it was time to "move on," as he had put it.

Scott was ruggedly handsome, with bright blue eyes, a boyish grin, and a head of thick, wavy auburn hair. All the women in the church noticed him. The single ones started dressing nicer for services, and Bible study never had so many attendees as when he was leading it. He was a charismatic preacher, and even the men thought he was great. He got many of them involved in projects around the church that they had never dreamed of doing before.

Jillian and Scott had worked together on a new food pantry project shortly after he arrived. She was definitely attracted to him, but tried to be very professional. Finally, one night he asked her to go to dinner with him after one of their meetings. They went to a place on the other side of the city so they wouldn't become an item of gossip. Marty was at a friend's house studying until she got home.

They began dating in secret over the next six months. There was nothing really against dating in the official church rules, but they felt that they would reveal their relationship when the right time came. They had serious discussions about how they must keep the "visions and expectations" of the church, which did not permit premarital relations for single leaders and required faithfulness to one's spouse if one was married.

Following the guidelines was an easy decision for Jillian. She had no intention of making that mistake again. She had learned her lesson after what had happened the first time. She also had a thirteen-year-old daughter to consider. She wanted to be the best role model she could possibly be for Marty.

Just when Jillian thought that she and Scott might become an "official" couple, her world collapsed. It was discovered that Scott, who had been adamant that they not sleep with one another, had been sleeping with numerous women in the congregation, both single and married. Later it was discovered that this had also occurred in his previous church after his wife had passed away. The congregation was shocked. Jillian was absolutely crushed.

Scott was removed from the pastoral roster of the denomination, and the last thing Jillian had heard, he was working at a wedding chapel in Atlantic City, New Jersey. She often thought he was lucky to be alive. He could have been shot by someone's angry husband. The congregation was scandalized and would not recover from this sad situation for years, and neither would Jillian.

Even though Jillian had not really done anything wrong, she felt she could not continue in her position as parish nurse in that church. She was hurt and humiliated. Everywhere she went, she was reminded of Scott and was also reminded that once again she had chosen poorly in the affairs of the heart. Scott had really fooled her, but then again, he had fooled a lot of people. He had talked so convincingly, so sincerely. Later she would go to counseling and find out that his behavior was common for those who did what he did.

After Scott was terminated, Jillian started to look for a new job right away. With a master's degree and years of experience, she had easily gotten a position with the University of Wisconsin Hospital and Clinics in Madison, and she and Marty moved once more. It had been a good move—great schools, a wonderful church, a top-notch hospital, and a beautiful city. She had forgotten how special Madison was, and it had only gotten better in the years since she had been an undergraduate student. Jillian had worked at the hospital until just a few months ago, having been there ten years. They were good years, filled with good work and good friends.

But over that ten years, she protected her heart like a hawk. The first two years after Scott, she refused to go out at all. She needed some time to heal. After that, she had gone on a few dates, usually as a favor to someone who needed a double date or to get someone who was bugging her to date off her back. But quite frankly, she didn't really feel that she wanted, or needed, to date. Marty was in high school, playing soccer, singing in choir, and performing in musicals. They had found a church that they enjoyed and were very active members. Life was full and busy. Honestly, Jillian didn't really feel that anything was missing in her life, and before she knew it, ten years had flown past.

Jillian's thoughts snapped back to the present as Karen asked her opinion on a good pair of walking shoes. They decided it would be easier if they went shopping together, so Karen drove them to a sporting shoes store, and Jillian helped her pick out her first pair of cross trainers. Jillian felt energized and happy. She was going to help her new friend get in better shape. In fact, maybe she would post her walking plan on her blog. That way, she could assuage the guilt she sometimes felt for leaving—"running away" may have been a better term—her position in parish nursing after the fiasco with Scott. Someday, she thought to herself, she would find some way to help people again like she had when she was in that position, even if it were only on a volunteer basis. In the meantime, Jillian needed to attend to her current life situations, both the personal and the professional.

❖

Jillian needed to take a ride to the library. The next book for her book club was *The House on Mango Street*. She had taken more and more books to the house for Mr. Romano to read, including what she considered the better young adult books, such as the *Harry Potter* and *The Hunger Games* series. The next selections on her list for Mr. Romano were *The Help* and *Gilead*, two books that she had personally enjoyed.

She left *The Help* out first. After a couple of days, she got an idea. She hoped that she didn't get fired for it, but she just *had* to do it. She would make a chocolate pie. In the book, a maid named Minnie was known for her delicious chocolate pies. Her employer loved these pies. The employer got angry with Minnie for something she did wrong and fired Minnie. Minnie pretended to act sorry for what she had done wrong and as a gesture of apology made the woman one of her pies, but this time with a special added *ingredient*, to get back at the woman. It was one of the more memorable parts of the book and later the movie based on the book.

Kathy J. Jacobson

Jillian rode to the store and got an aluminum pie tin, the kind that comes with its own plastic cover, and some evaporated milk. She had the rest of the ingredients in her cupboard. That night she mixed everything together in a large bowl and poured it into the pie tin. She baked it for fifty minutes and then let it cool on a wire rack. The recipe said it was best when it was at room temperature. She would put that on the note.

She couldn't wait to put the pie in the refrigerator the next afternoon. She only hoped that Mr. Romano had a sense of humor about this. She had now almost doubled her record time for employment in the household. Mr. Mack was so pleased that he gave her a bonus on her last pay deposit. That was nice of him, she thought, though not necessary. She was enjoying the busywork, had made new friends, loved her cottage, was riding her new bike, and writing on a regular basis. She was even beginning to outline the chapters that would one day become the book that would tie all her blog posts and other thoughts together.

Four-thirty finally came, and into the refrigerator went "Minnie's Pie." She didn't call it that. That was part of the point, for him to figure it out, which she had no doubt that he would if he had read the book. If he hadn't read it, he could just enjoy a delicious pie. She placed the pie, baked in the disposable tin, in the refrigerator and wrote her note—perhaps her last one, she thought with a bit of wariness. On the other hand, Mr. Romano may not acknowledge it at all, because that would let her know that he was indeed reading the books that she left on the counter. That made her feel a little bit better as she scribbled the words.

There is a special dessert for you in the refrigerator.
The recipe says it tastes best served at room temperature.

The sky looked ominous, like a storm was brewing, so she went back to her cottage and began reading her new book club book.

She couldn't wait to become lost in the next new world that awaited her. This time, it would be a small house on street in a crowded Latino neighborhood in Chicago, the new home of a girl named Esperanza.

Jillian read for two hours, then put the novel down so she could do some writing of her own. She thought that after she wrote her book to help those with broken hearts, she would try her hand at a novel. It could still help others with broken hearts, she thought, but just in a different way.

❖

The next morning Jillian felt nervous as she dressed for the day. *That chocolate pie may not have been your brightest move, Jillian.* She was not sure what she would find when she arrived at work. She brought along the library book, *Gilead,* thinking it may serve as a peace offering.

She tentatively opened the door to the kitchen. She had taken *The Help* back with her the previous day, so there had only been her note left there, written on a piece of yellow notepaper. Now there appeared to be a turquoise-colored note left on the counter. Hers was gone, so there was no doubt that he had read it.

She couldn't decide if she should look at the note first or the refrigerator. She really didn't care if he had eaten any pie or dumped it this time. She just didn't want to be in the unemployment line tomorrow.

She opted to go for the note. There was just one word on it, written in capital letters with an exclamation point.

NOTED!

It was the exact same message she had written to him two months before, which she had angrily written after the pilau dumping incident. She hoped he wasn't too upset with her. She wondered if he had thrown the pie away, but when she checked the refrigerator, the pie tin was there—with a piece missing. He couldn't have been too angry if he had eaten a piece of the pie and kept the rest, and she realized that by his response, he had just admitted he was reading the books she left on the counter. She smiled to herself as she closed the refrigerator door.

Chapter Nine

It was springtime in California. Actually, to Jillian, it had felt like springtime ever since she had arrived. But everywhere she went—the store, the library, her book club, church—the native Californians kept telling her it was *finally* spring.

Part of the reason Jillian loved this time of year was the return of more daylight. A couple of minutes at the beginning and end of each day seemed to add up quickly. In the Midwest, she had also appreciated how it had gradually gotten warmer during these months, albeit *warmer* was a relative term. The snow would finally start to melt, and the crocuses would push up from the ground, sometimes right through the snow. In her current locale, the warmth wasn't as much of the issue to her. Everything seemed toasty to her compared to what she had experienced for the last twelve years. But the extra daylight—that was a gift—no matter where one lived.

❖

It was the Lenten season at church, one of her favorite seasons. She enjoyed the evening midweek church services and the contemplative nature of the season. The only drawback Jillian could see this year would be that she would be missing a couple of book club meetings, which were unfortunately on Wednesday nights. She would have to get the titles from Karen and read the books on her own. They could have their own discussions about them, she decided.

She and Karen were spending more and more time together. Karen was a thoughtful and bright woman, but it seemed clear that she needed to find more productive and meaningful ways to use her skills. Jillian hoped that she might help her discover what some of those ways could be.

Drew, however, was another story. Jillian was running out of good excuses for not going out with him. As a favor, she had recently consented to go to a last-minute cocktail party with him, hosted by one of his clients. It was three hours of boring small-talk and "one-upmanship," and Jillian couldn't wait for the evening to be over. Otherwise, she didn't see much of Drew outside of church and the book club.

Drew and Jillian weren't much for talking on the phone. They had so little in common that it was difficult sometimes to come up with more than just generic conversation when in person, let alone over the phone, especially now that they knew each other better and had shared their stories with one another. Drew, however, kept trying to keep the dating relationship going, although Jillian was not certain why he was going to so much trouble. It was clear, at least to her, that there was no real future for them as a couple.

On the work front, Jillian decided to be bold once again. After she was fairly certain that Mr. Romano had read *Gilead,* she wrote a note that said:

What did you think?

The next day he wrote back:

I didn't care for the ending.

Jillian was surprised, because that was her exact reaction to the book as well. She wasn't certain what possessed her, but she wrote back a response, using two pieces of notepaper and very small print, which basically said how she would have written the ending, if it had been up to her.

Mr. Romano wrote back:

Interesting.

Coming from a man who had read thousands of books, who was a literature major, and who rarely responded to anything or anybody, this made Jillian feel like she had just won a Pulitzer. She took the note and put it in her pocket, like it was some kind of prize. She went on to clean the five bathrooms, humming as she went about her day.

Jillian blogged that evening about small miracles. She was so excited that she had had some sort of response from Mr. Romano, and a positive one at that.

Later, she couldn't sleep. She stood up and glanced at the window. She just couldn't help it. She walked slowly to the window and turned the blinds to see if the kitchen light was on. She hadn't done that in months. Sure enough, there was Mr. Romano just closing *Memoirs of a Geisha,* the latest library book she had left for him. She watched him take off his reading glasses. He set the book down on the counter, but this time he didn't try to make it look like he hadn't read it. *Progress!*

Jillian still wished, however, that he would talk to someone—anyone. The phone rang several times every week, and he never picked it up. Sometimes it was the annoyed voice of his agent, who wanted him to do an audition. But most of the time, the calls were from his nephew, Tommy. She would hear the pain in his voice on the answering machine as he would plead with his uncle to please call. It hurt Jillian's heart.

But maybe now, she thought, he was finally on the right track. He was actually answering notes, and in positive ways. She had the feeling that this was going to be a slow process, however. But she knew that healing was often just that—a very slow process. So, as she climbed back into her cozy bed, she said her usual prayers, and then thanked God for the small miracles going on in Mr. Romano's life—and hers.

Chapter Ten

Jillian knew it had to happen sooner or later. Sometime she was going to meet the animal that Mr. Mack had referred to as "the beast," and this was the day. It was a Friday afternoon. Jillian was in the kitchen getting ingredients out to make dinner, when a flash of orange ran into the room. She could hear Mr. Romano calling in another part of the house, "Lu - cy! Lu - cy!"

The orange short-haired cat stopped dead in her tracks when she saw Jillian. She didn't look like a beast to Jillian, so Jillian just said, "Hello, kitty," in a kind, gentle voice. At that, the cat walked up to her, sniffed her, and then started rubbing up against her legs.

Jillian slowly reached down to pet her. Now the cat started to purr. This animal didn't seem like a beast to Jillian. She wondered if she dare pick her up. Slowly and gently, she picked her up, hugging her to her chest, just as she had often done with the untamed barn cats when she was a kid.

Rubbing the cat behind the ears, she continued the conversation. "Lucy, huh? That's a perfect name for a kitty with bright orange hair," Jillian said softly to her. The cat was purring away as Jillian touched her soft fur. The animal even smelled good. Lucy was meticulously groomed, and Jillian was certain that she was brushed each and every day.

She was so absorbed in petting the cat that she didn't see Mr. Romano enter the room until she heard him say, "Lu...." Just like his cat, he stopped dead in his tracks, especially at the sight of Jillian holding Lucy.

Jillian and Mr. Romano just looked at one another for a moment. It was the first time they had ever been in the same room together. It was the first time they had ever seen each other face-to-face. Jillian could feel blood rushing to her cheeks, but she tried to focus on the animal in her arms.

"Is this who you're looking for?" Jillian asked, continuing to stroke the purring feline and smiling.

"Yes...." He seemed to be at a loss for words. He was probably in shock, seeing his cat on friendly terms with one of the "helpers," rather than being swatted with a broom or causing major damage to someone's skin or clothing.

He just stared. "Lucy, come here," he finally said.

Jillian gently set her down on the floor. The cat once again wound herself around Jillian's ankles. Jillian petted her one last time and told her, "You'd better go, Lucy. It was nice to meet you."

As if the cat understood everything Jillian had said, she sauntered over to Mr. Romano. He picked her up, petting her gently.

"Thank you," he said quietly and turned to leave the room.

"You are most welcome. She's a nice cat. Perfect name, too," Jillian said.

"Yes...well...good afternoon," he said and walked out of the room.

Jillian's heart was pounding. She supposed she was all flushed, too. She could usually speak like she was under perfect control, but unfortunately she never could keep her physiology in check in stressful situations.

Mr. Romano had seemed taller and stronger in "real life" than she had expected. Of course, she had only seen him on a television screen or from a distance previously. *He did play college football, Jillian.* His broad shoulders and his hands definitely looked like they belonged to someone who had been a quarterback, although the players from his playing era were not as big as many of today's players.

Jillian had worked a rotation at University Hospital with some of the young athletes undergoing surgeries, usually football players with knee problems. Some of them were gargantuan. Thinking of those players and their injuries made her think about Mr. Romano's knee again. His limp seemed more pronounced than it had when she watched him walk away from the pool that morning months before. And she thought he had seemed a bit unsteady as he turned to leave the room. She decided that if they ever got to a point at which they spoke more than a word or two to one another, she would encourage him to see an orthopedic specialist. But that, she was quite certain, was a long way off, if ever. Their accidental meeting may have been their first, and only, meeting.

Jillian felt flustered the rest of that day. She made Mr. Romano's dinner, just as ordered. She thought any deviations might be too much after the face-to-face sighting of one another. She sincerely hoped that she was not in trouble for picking up the cat. It sounded like people had been fired for a lot less than that. She also remembered Mr. Mack saying that Mr. Romano did not want to *see* the "helpers"—ever. And she had not only been seen, but she had actually dared to speak to him.

❖

As soon as her work was done, Jillian went back to the cottage to change, then went to the garage to grab her bike. She needed to ride some tension out. A short hour later, she headed home. She would have ridden longer, but she was famished. She grabbed an apple and then her cell phone. For whatever reason, she suddenly felt like she needed to get out of there—and now.

She called Karen.

"Hi, Karen! What are you up to tonight?" Jillian asked. Karen had often complained to her that she was home alone a lot, and the two of them had talked about going out some weekend evening.

"You'll never believe what I did today," Karen said. "I called my husband at work and told him I had two tickets to the Lakers game tonight, and that I was going one way or the other, and hoped he would join me...and he said, 'yes!'"

Karen sounded so excited that it made Jillian smile for her friend.

"I never would have done something like that before I met you, Jillian," Karen continued.

"I don't know about that, Karen. I don't think I can take the credit for that."

"Well, all I know is that I'm doing all kinds of new things lately—walking, baking, and I just signed up for an online class. It's just a basic college English class. I'm going to see how I do, and if all goes well, I might try to finish my degree. And it was your example that encouraged me. Just your story of moving out here and trying to become a writer—it's so daring. You're an inspiration, Jillian."

Jillian did not feel very inspirational at that moment, but she was very happy for Karen.

"I think Robert was in shock when I called him, and he said yes before he really had time to think about it. I got the idea from you—or from your mom, I guess. I remembered you telling me how you would be all ready to go to town, and she would tell your dad that you were going to do something, with or without him. So, that's what I did!"

Jillian had forgotten she had told Karen about that. She smiled again, thinking that her mom would have appreciated the fact that her tactics still worked.

Karen continued, "The most important thing is that he is going. *We* are going! Robert said he's coming home early to change and that we should try to get there early to watch the team warm-up. So, I've got to go. Was there something you wanted to talk about, Jillian?"

"It can wait until another time, Karen. Have a wonderful time with Robert tonight!"

"I sure hope so. Jillian...uh...I've never asked anyone to do such a thing before, but will you pray for us tonight?"

"You can count on it," Jillian said with an even bigger smile on her face.

The call ended. Jillian was overjoyed for her new friend, but that didn't change the way she felt at the moment, and the smile faded from her face. She didn't feel she could stay on the premises that evening.

Next she placed a call to Nancy from church. She was a widow and was always saying how busy her family was and that she rarely saw them. Perhaps she needed some companionship that evening. But when Jillian called, Nancy explained that one of her sons had dropped in unexpectedly. She was making him his favorite meal, and he was working on a few of the items on her "to-do list" around the house. Nancy sounded ecstatic, and Jillian again felt happy for another new friend.

Jillian just sat for a moment. She knew she probably shouldn't do it, but she pressed the contact on her phone for Drew. He was still at the office and sounded thrilled that she called. They decided to go to a movie. That sounded fun, and pretty *safe* to Jillian.

A small wave of guilt washed over her that she was using Drew and giving him false hope, but she was very happy to be doing anything—anywhere—with anyone that evening. She wasn't sure why she felt that way, but the feeling was overwhelming.

Kathy J. Jacobson

They ended up going to see what Jillian would term a "war movie." It wouldn't have been Jillian's first choice, but she felt like she owed it to Drew to let him choose the movie. It was actually an interesting true story, and well-acted. She decided she would have to read the book it was based on to see how it compared.

After the movie, they slipped into a small booth that had just been vacated at a nearby bistro and had a glass of wine and an appetizer. The place had a mellow feel about it, and the wine took some of the edge off Jillian's nerves. Drew was talking about his parents and the trip they were planning to take to Europe, or at least his mother was planning. They would be gone for two weeks. His father was having an absolute fit about being gone from the firm so long, but Drew's mother had insisted on the trip, and his father had finally, and reluctantly, agreed. Jillian was beginning to understand more and more how Drew had acquired his workaholic habits. She was happy for Drew's mother, the second woman she had learned about that day who had "put her foot down."

All in all, it was a fairly enjoyable evening. Drew was on his best behavior, sensing that this was an opportunity to get his foot back in the door with Jillian. He was a perfect gentleman when he dropped her off this time. He hurried around the SUV to open her door for her, but there was no grabbing and kissing this time. He just hugged her gently and said goodnight.

Jillian felt grateful—for the evening out and especially for the polite goodnight. She wasn't in the mood to be grabbed and kissed. At least she didn't think she was. *Not by Drew anyway.*

As she crossed the shadowy yard, she glanced at the house to see if Mr. Romano was reading tonight, but it was completely dark. What Jillian hadn't noticed, however, was Mr. Romano peering down from the corner of the front window of his bedroom suite when Drew dropped her off in front of the house. Nor did she see him standing in the shadows of the suite's balcony as she made her way back to the cottage through the backyard.

Once inside, she kicked off her shoes and fell into her bed, still fully clothed. Jillian grabbed her pillow into a hug. Why did she feel so strange tonight? She couldn't put her finger on it. She fell asleep on the bed, waking up at two a.m., her clothes feeling tight and binding. She quickly changed and went back to bed. She lay there a moment and stared at the ceiling. For the first time in a very long time, Jillian felt like something was missing in her life. She fell back to sleep, hoping the feeling would be gone the next day.

❖

Drew called the very next morning. *Here we go. You really opened up a can of worms, Jillian.* But since the odd feeling from the evening before was still nagging her, she decided she was just going to "go with it," whatever "it" was. Drew announced that he was free for the day and asked it there was something she would like to do.

She wanted to do something new. After reading *The House on Mango Street,* she said she would really like to go to Olvera Street, in the oldest area of Los Angeles. She knew it was a bit touristy, but she was not from L.A. She wanted to learn about the city she now called home. But Drew sounded so hesitant about going there that she changed her mind. She had no intention of going to a place with someone who wouldn't appreciate it or didn't want to be there.

She felt like being outside, so next she asked, "How about Disneyland?"

"That's for kids," was Drew's response.

Jillian did not agree. Shortly after her father was diagnosed with cancer, he had announced that they were all going to Florida and to Disney World. Marty was only four, but old enough to enjoy the experience. Jillian and her parents—well, they enjoyed it even more than Marty had. It was truly a magical kingdom and a trip she would never forget.

Jillian was not in the mood to argue, so she asked him for other suggestions.

"We could do the Getty Center."

"That would be great, as long as we spend at least sometime outside in the gardens, as well as the museum. I do want to see the '*Irises*.'"

"I'm not sure that they have irises growing there right now, but maybe," Drew said.

"No... I mean, they may have irises growing in the gardens, but I was referring to the painting by Van Gogh." When she and Marty had been "on holiday" in St. Remy, in the Provence region of France, they learned how Vincent Van Gogh had spent the final years of his life in an insane asylum there. During that time, he painted many flower paintings, the *Irises* among them. It was one of Jillian's favorite paintings, perhaps because her family had had irises of all different colors growing on a small hill near the barn on their small family farm. The irises, along with some peonies, were the first blooms on their property each year. When they began to bloom, it meant that summer was finally near.

Jillian and Drew split their time between the gardens and the museum, with a light lunch in between at the cafe on the premises. The place was stunning—and huge. One would have to come back many times to see and appreciate it all. Jillian looked down on the center of the gardens from a deck above. It reminded her of a labyrinth. She wished it were. Right then, she felt like she needed to walk a labyrinth and engage in some serious prayer.

Inside the museum, she and Drew eventually worked their way to the painting of the *Irises*. She had seen a photo of it in a book, but seeing it in real life was very special. As she gazed at it, one thing really jumped out at her. It was the single white iris, in among all the colorful ones.

"That's him," she said aloud, mostly to herself, but Drew heard her.

"What are you talking about?" he asked.

"That white iris—I think it's Van Gogh. I think he knew he was going to be dead soon, or perhaps he already felt dead inside, as much as he didn't fit into this world, and as depressed as he was."

Jillian went on to express to Drew how sad she thought it was that a person suffering from depression in 1889 could only find help in an asylum for the insane. In actuality, he was probably more sane that the vast majority of people alive at his time. She thought about her favorite line from *Don Quixote:* "Too much sanity is insanity." She often thought that geniuses, like Van Gogh and so many others, had too much sanity. They could see things other people could never see. They could understand things in ways others couldn't come close to comprehending. They could feel things that others couldn't. She thought it must be a very lonely and tortured existence to go through life like that, and Jillian believed it was why so many exceptional people ended their own lives.

"Humph," was all that Drew could muster.

At that moment, it appeared obvious to Jillian that Drew and Vincent Van Gogh—as well as Drew and she—had very little in common.

"Are you ready to go?" Drew asked.

"I'd like to stop in the gift shop for a bit, then we can go."

Jillian bought a magnet with the *Irises* on it. She had thought seriously about a print or a poster she could have framed, but she wasn't sure what she would do with it at this point. She didn't really want to hang anything up in the cottage.

She also bought three postcards of the painting. She would keep one as a souvenir. One she would send to Marty in remembrance of their trip to France. She wasn't sure what she would do with the other one yet. She almost put it back, but decided she would buy it and think about it some more.

The rest of Jillian's weekend was filled with church, biking, and writing in her blog. Her blog post discussed dating someone with whom one has little in common. Was it a good idea to continue in such a relationship, or was it a mistake? That was her question to her readers. She gave some of her thoughts—the pluses and minuses according to Jillian, and others chimed in.

There was no real consensus out there, and there was no consensus in Jillian's mind either, so she decided to let things go on as they were with Drew, at least for the time being. She promised herself that if Drew seemed to become too serious, she would have to call things to a halt. She wouldn't want to hurt him. In the meantime, they both seemed to appreciate each other on some level. But she still sometimes got that feeling that everything Drew did was about business in some way, and if not about business, about Drew.

As Jillian got ready for bed that night, one post by one of her blog followers haunted her. The person said that often people date people they *know* things will not work out with, because those people are "*safe.*" The problem with these safe relationships, the person said, is that they keep people from getting into a true, meaningful, a.k.a. risky relationship, with someone with whom they could actually fall in love. Jillian had sighed when she read that one earlier. And she sighed again as her head hit the pillow. Because she knew in her heart, that the person was so very right.

❖

Jillian made it through the weekend without being fired for being seen by Mr. Romano, petting his cat, and speaking directly to him. That was a good thing. It was a typical Monday until she got back from lunch. Mr. Romano had been out of the house that morning to take Lucy on their usual run to the pet store, his only connection with the outside world to her knowledge. But this time, he must have made another stop.

There, on the counter was a box containing a fancy jar of hand cream with a note that said:

Thought you might like this.

Normally, Jillian would be thrilled by someone giving her an unexpected gift, but she felt a jolt of embarrassment. She had often been sensitive about her "nurse's hands," as she called them. All the soap and water, hand sanitizer, and rubber gloves could really take their toll on them.

One time she had been walking in a mall in Milwaukee, when one of the center aisle vendors hawking hand and face products had called out to Jillian.

"Why do you wash your hands so much? Are you a nurse?" the woman practically shouted at her, spotting the roughness and redness of Jillian's hands even from a distance.

Jillian had come to a screeching halt. She had been stunned. She couldn't imagine anyone asking—so loudly—such a rude question to a complete stranger, as this woman had just done.

"Actually, I *am* a nurse. And a mother. And *you* are?" It may have been one of her rudest responses ever to anyone, and of course she felt terrible about it later.

"Never mind," the saleswoman had said, and Jillian had gone on her way, her face a flaming scarlet. Ever since, she had been self-conscious about her hands. And now, in her one very brief encounter with Mr. Romano, her hands must have stood out again. She had thought they were looking a bit better lately. The cleaning and rubber gloves were still tough on them, but not as bad as nursing had been. Obviously, they still had a long way to go.

She had the urge to just let the package sit there, but then again, that would be rude, too. She reluctantly took it back with her at the end of the day and left a note with one word.

Thanks.

When Jillian got back to the cottage, she put the jar down on the table by the TV and her laptop. She was scheduled for a video call with Marty and couldn't wait. She got a glass of water for herself and then just stared at her laptop until she heard it "ring."

Jillian told her daughter about meeting Mr. Romano and his cat, then Jillian unloaded to her daughter about the unexpected "gift." She also told Marty that Mr. Mack mentioned during their initial meeting that Mr. Romano had one helper walk off the job because she was overweight and he had left her some type of herbal weight loss supplement. The helper had been so offended that she quit her job that very day, after only a week on the job.

Marty, as usual, tried to put the most positive spin on the situation. Jillian had told her the name of the cream and that at least it came in beautiful jar. Marty was near another computer at the time and typed the product name into the search engine.

"Mom. You know that hand cream you are complaining about?"

"Yes, what about it?"

"According to this website, it has excellent reviews. And it should, because it costs about $200 per ounce."

"*What*?"

"You heard me right. That is a pretty nice present you have there."

Now Jillian felt like a heel, even worse than she had when she had been rude to that mall vendor years ago.

"Mom, did you ever consider that Mr. Romano was trying to be helpful when he left you that cream? Or even when he left that other helper that weight loss supplement because she needed to lose some weight? He may not be too hot in the tact department, but I think there's a good chance that he was just trying to be nice—in his own way."

"I think there's a very good chance that you are exactly right," said Jillian. She thought back to some of the practical gifts that her dad used to give her mom for Christmas, her birthday, Mother's Day, and even Valentine's Day. She once asked her mom if she minded getting those kinds of gifts. Her mom had told her she didn't mind because she knew her dad was doing his best at picking them out and trying to buy things that would make her life easier. Her mom had said once, "He's not very romantic, but he's very loving. And that in its own way, is very romantic."

Jillian told Marty what her Mom had said long ago.

"That is so sweet. I miss Grandma," Marty said.

"Me, too," Jillian said.

It had been years since her death, but there were so many times Jillian wished she could just call her mom and ask for her thoughts.

Jillian and Marty talked about Marty's week, which was quieter than usual. Jillian told her to relish those quiet times—they were few and far between. Per usual, after they said goodbye, Jillian wondered what she had ever done to deserve that girl, and what she would ever do without her.

Jillian closed her laptop and picked up the box that came with the hand cream. She read the small informational pamphlet that came with it. Later that night, after she was done brushing her teeth and washing her face, she tried out the cream. It felt luxurious. *It should for that price!* Then she wondered if she should had even accepted something so costly, but something in her heart said that it was the right thing to do.

Chapter Eleven

It was the week before Easter. There were a lot of church services to attend during Holy Week. Jillian loved them, but especially looked forward to the happy and glorious celebration on Easter Sunday.

The weather had been glorious, too. Jillian had been bike riding nearly every day and now had a few set routes. On one of them, she ran into the young mother, Meredith, and little Charlie again. The woman seemed happy to stop and talk this time, although she was preoccupied with the baby, who seemed to continually fuss. Jillian had had to cut their little street visit short, as she had to get back home and get ready for church.

"You go to *church*?" the young woman had said, sounding amazed.

"Yes, I do. Every Sunday usually, and this week, a lot more than that."

The woman had looked like she was thinking, but didn't say anything else. She bent down to try to soothe the baby.

"He cries all the time, Jillian, and he is always spitting up—a lot. The doctor said it is colic, but I still worry."

"When is his next checkup, Meredith?"

"Not for another three weeks."

"Colic is one thing, but it could be something else, especially with that spitting up." The baby didn't seem to be overly thriving when she looked at him again. "If he doesn't seem better by Easter, or if he seems to get worse even before that, take him in."

Meredith thanked her and wished her a happy Easter. Jillian liked the young woman, who, like so many people she met in this affluent neighborhood, seemed lonely and not very happy.

❖

It looked like the bike riding bug was contagious. Early the next day, when Jillian had taken the trash to the garage, Mr. Romano's bike was down from the hooks and standing in the garage. It was the first time she had ever seen it on the ground. A helmet sat on the seat, and the tires looked pumped with air and ready to roll. She felt excited for her employer. It was a positive sign that he was thinking of engaging in an activity, and a healthy one at that.

But later that afternoon, the "bug" got squashed. Jillian was cleaning a smudge off the window in one of the bedrooms facing the front yard, when she happened to glance down the driveway, just in time to witness a very unhappy and disturbing sight.

Mr. Romano, dressed in biking clothing, was walking a crumpled bike from the street to the curb at the end of the driveway. He threw the bike down angrily, then took off his helmet and threw it on top of the bike, leaving them both for the trash collectors. She could see that his leg was bleeding, and his arm and elbow, too. Thank goodness he had been wearing a helmet.

She wondered what had happened, but then she remembered his knee and how unsteady he had been as he had turned to leave the room the one time they had seen each other in person. He really needed to go to a doctor and have that knee checked.

He's going to be sore later, she thought to herself, the nurse in her coming out. She started worrying about his pain management, too, and sincerely hoped he didn't have any old prescription drugs laying around in a drawer somewhere to tempt him. And she hoped he would clean his wounds well. She wanted to rush down to him and start treating his wounds, but didn't dare.

She was finished cleaning the bedroom, but decided to wait until she heard him come into the house and she could detect where he was heading before she made a move. She didn't want to run into him and cause him further humiliation. She only wished that she could help him in some way.

She heard his footsteps on the stairs, then heard the door to his bedroom suite slam shut. She quickly picked up her cleaning supplies and tiptoed down the stairs.

Jillian put her supplies away, making as little noise as possible. She was done for the day, having made a chicken salad that was already in the refrigerator. She decided she had to write him a note. Correction—notes. She gave Mr. Romano instructions on how to clean the wounds and what to do/not do if he had injured his head, just in case he had sustained a concussion. She told him to get some antibiotic ointment, if he didn't already have some, and to use ice and ibuprofen for pain and swelling. She also gave him some brief, simple meditation techniques that were useful for pain management. There were a lot of notes left that night. Maybe this time she'd get fired, but she felt she had to do something.

The next morning, there was a note for her.

what do you think you are—a doctor?

She wrote back to him.

No, that would be my daughter. I'm a nurse.
B.S.N. University of Wisconsin
M.S.N. Marquette University

She wished she could see the wounds and know that he was okay, but she knew that wasn't going to happen. She put the pen down and reluctantly headed to the cottage to get ready for that evening's church service.

That night, she sat with Nancy and some new friends, Sam and Ruth. On this night, the story of the "Last Supper" was recalled. She knew it well, and she knew what would come next. She thought about all the pain and humiliation.

She couldn't help it. Thinking about pain and humiliation made her think of Mr. Romano. The bike accident was the *last* thing he needed. Just when he was trying to do something constructive, something he hadn't done in a long time, it ended in an embarrassing, painful mess. She worried about his depressive behavior and wondered if this was going to set him back again to where he had been, or even worse. During the prayers of the people that evening, she said a prayer out loud for those suffering their own pain and humiliation on this night. And she said a silent prayer specifically for Mr. Romano.

❖

There was no response the next day to her list of credentials. That was okay with her. What would Mr. Romano say anyway? As her week of work ended, Jillian left a library book on the counter and some hard-boiled eggs she had dyed in the refrigerator.

After work, she got ready for the Good Friday church service. She thought about how tired Pastor Jim must be. He had had a funeral earlier in the week on top of all the special services. On Easter morning, there would be three services instead of two. She hoped he was taking a vacation afterward. She actually felt like it might be time to think about taking one of her two paid weeks off herself. Not yet, she thought, but sometime soon.

She sat with Drew and Nancy at this service. It was a special service, with many readings and hymns. After each hymn, a candle was extinguished. Pastor Jim gave a brief reflection and prayer afterward, then they all left in silence.

Drew tried to talk to her inside the church, but she just headed for the door. *He could at least wait until we get outside of the doors.*

"Want to go out?" he asked.

"Not tonight, Drew. Sorry. Another time?"

"I suppose. I'll call you."

She was happy they were at a stage where she could just be honest with him. She did not feel like going out. Instead, Jillian went home. For some reason, she felt like she had to watch an episode of *O.R.* She picked one of her favorites, but later wished she hadn't watched it. For some reason, it made her feel even sadder than she had before. She guessed it was just the day. Soon it would be Easter. She needed Easter.

She was going to Easter dinner at Karen and Robert's house at two o'clock, so she decided to attend the eleven o'clock church service. She hoped, too, that she could get home in time to ride her bike. She hadn't gone out the last two days. It had been busy with the church services, but she also didn't feel like riding her bicycle in front of Mr. Romano right now. It would almost be like rubbing salt in a wound.

She had bought herself a new spring dress for church and the dinner. She hadn't had a new Easter dress in a long time. It made her feel good, and even though the day was a bit overcast, it couldn't dampen her spirits. It was Easter, and she felt like her optimism had been resurrected. She called a taxi and waited at the top of the drive.

The church service was joyful and packed, and dinner at the Wilsons was exceptional. Karen was excited to cook for company and pulled out all the stops. Robert seemed very proud of his wife. Karen had told her that ever since they went on that date to watch the Lakers, their relationship had improved tremendously. Robert was making an effort to come home at a more reasonable time each day, and they had gone on a few more "dates" since the game.

Karen had also started her online class and was enjoying it, even though it was just a basic course. Now she was looking for the right school and program to enroll in to finish her degree. Robert seemed proud of her for going back to school, too.

Jillian went home feeling better than she had in weeks. It really did feel like a day of new life and new beginnings, just the way it should on Easter Sunday, on Resurrection Day.

Jillian was able to sneak in a short bike ride when she returned home, which was a good thing after all the rich food she had eaten at Karen's. The day was topped off with a video chat with Marty. Jillian filled her in about Mr. Romano's accident and his discarding of his bike and helmet. Marty shared her concern about a possible setback and was truly sorry to hear about the accident. She said she would put him on her prayer chain in Senegal.

On a brighter note, Jillian told her the details of the church services, her new spring dress, and the wonderful meal she had shared with her friends for Easter dinner. Marty had been able to go to a service, too, and about two dozen people gathered for an Easter potluck dinner. Someone had even brought dyed eggs.

They talked until Marty had to get ready for work, as Monday morning was approaching in her world. Jillian, whose first Easter in California was coming to a close, was planning to post in her blog about new beginnings. She felt a lot like she had four months earlier, when she had first landed in Los Angeles International Airport. She was energized. She was renewed. She felt ready for anything.

Chapter Twelve

S ummer settled into Los Angeles a bit ahead of the summer
solstice, and Jillian finally found something she didn't care for
in her new home area. Smog. It was a nuisance, to say the least.
She was very happy that she did not have any chronic respiratory
ailments and wondered how people who did were able to live in
L.A., especially at this time of the year. The smog was actually
there all year round, but it was more pronounced on the warmer
summer days.

Jillian found it best to walk or ride her bike very early in the
morning, if at all. She missed the rides and also some of the people she had started to run into on a regular basis. She had seen
Meredith and her baby, Charlie, the week after Easter. Meredith
told her that she had been waiting with the baby on a corner for
Jillian a few days in a row, hoping that she would ride by.

"You were right, Jillian. There was something wrong with Charlie. There was a little muscle that wasn't working properly and was
making him spit up all the time. He was starting to lose weight
and not getting his nutrients. The doctors fixed it easily enough
the day after Easter, but if you hadn't told me to take him in, he

would have continued to suffer until things were really bad. The doctor said that it was good that we brought him in when we did. Thank you so much," Meredith said and even hugged her. After that, they met a few more times on the street until the summer weather set in.

Jillian missed her regular exercise routine, so she decided that the wisest thing to do was to join a gym for a few months. She had often done that in the dead of winter in the Midwest. In Los Angeles, it was the exact opposite. Summer was going to be her new gym time.

She did find that going to the beach was a good idea, too, as the breezes coming off the Pacific improved the air quality nearby. The only drawback was the crowd that had the same idea as she did on the weekends, so sometimes it made that idea less appealing.

The gym she joined was not too far from her house. When it was a better air quality day, she rode her bike. Her first day at the facility, she wished she hadn't ridden, as she was pretty sore from some of the new exercises. She should have known better. The next day, she took a taxi, deciding she would ride her bike only after her muscles were more adjusted to her new workout routine, provided there was actually another clear day.

As a bonus for signing up, she was granted one session with a personal trainer, and she was meeting with the person today. She hadn't asked for any particular trainer and wasn't certain that it really mattered if the trainer was male or female, younger or older.

She went to the desk and told the young woman behind it that she was there for her session.

"Oh, I'm sorry," the woman said. "We tried to call you, but you didn't answer. Your trainer, Barbara, is ill today, and we will have to reschedule."

"No, you won't," said a very deep male voice from behind the young woman. A gentleman in his early to mid-thirties, who looked like he could be a Mr. America candidate, had just approached the desk from an office behind it.

"I can do your session, if you don't mind," he said to Jillian.

"No, I don't mind," Jillian said. *Are you kidding? I don't think there is a female in this room who would mind.*

"Pete," the man said, extending his huge, strong hand to shake hers.

"Jillian," she said, firmly shaking his hand. Her hand felt like a baby's hand in his, and she was grateful for her new hand cream, which really did work. *Marty, you should be here right now.* She thought that her daughter could appreciate this situation much more than she could and that Pete could appreciate her twenty-five-year-old daughter much more as well.

Pete asked her if she had any specific goals or areas she would like to focus on. She told him her goal was to get a good cardio workout and keep her muscles toned during the smog season. She told him how she usually biked an hour or more a day, but that it was more difficult and not that healthy for her lungs to do that right now.

He agreed and showed her how to use some machines, giving her some recommendations on times and reps she should start with and build up to. He was such a pleasant man, very upbeat and very patient. She appreciated both of those qualities.

Their hour-long session zoomed by, then he left her to do some cool-down exercises. Jillian was very happy that she had not brought her bike. She could tell she was going ache after the new exercises.

Jillian went back to the women's locker room after her cool-down to shower and change. On her way out of the gym, she stopped just inside the front door and called for a taxi on her phone. She didn't see Pete heading toward her. He must have overheard her saying she needed a taxi, because for the second time that day he said, "No, you won't."

"Won't what?" she asked, looking at him with her cell phone to her ear.

"Need a taxi. I can give you a ride...if you'd like."

Jillian was flabbergasted. "I...I...guess I don't need a taxi after all," she said to the person on the other end of the line. She ended the call and put her phone in her bag.

"Where to?" Pete asked.

She told him the address.

"Ooh, pretty swanky."

"It is, but I don't own it, unfortunately. I live in the guest cottage. I am a live-in household helper for an agency. And an aspiring writer."

"Cool," Pete said as he opened the door for her. She appreciated his manners and also his comment, and she could tell that he really meant it.

On the way home, Jillian told Pete about how she had moved out to L.A. at the beginning of the year, gotten the job, and her thoughts thus far about her new home.

"That is really brave of you, leaving a job like nursing. But I totally get where you're coming from. I was a banker for a brief time. I couldn't stand it. I had to do something different. The only place I felt like a human being was at the gym, so I started looking into programs for personal training, and voila, here I am. That was seven years ago. I think I put the years back onto my life that I lost while I was working in the bank. Best move I ever made."

"Good for you, Pete. Too many people stay in jobs they don't like, or even bad relationships, because it's the easy thing to do rather than listening to their hearts. And you are right. A lot of times it takes years off their lives. I've seen it many times over."

"I'll bet you have."

The trip home went very quickly. Pete drove up to the top of the driveway. He hopped out of his Honda CRV and came around to open the door for Jillian.

"Thank you, Pete. And thanks for the ride and the training session. You'll have me in shape in no time at all," she said with a smile.

"You're already in good shape, but I know I can help you feel even stronger and stay in shape for the summer—smog season—wasn't that how you put it? That's funny," he said, smiling with his perfect teeth, their whiteness accentuated by his tanned skin.

"Well, thanks again. See you at the gym," she replied.

"Yeah, see ya," he said and hopped back into his vehicle. He watched her go through the gate and then drove off.

What just happened? Jillian headed back to her cottage and collapsed into one of the soft chairs. *That was interesting.* She thought about the muscle-bound Pete. Even his muscles had muscles. And he was sweet, and funny, and brave to leave a banking job to become a personal trainer. She could really appreciate his story.

She made herself a salad and put some leftover grilled salmon on it. She had purchased a small, portable gas grill for her little patio. It had been one of her better buys. She sat out on the patio and ate, feeling sore yet great at the same time. She always loved the way her muscles felt after a good workout, unless she really had overdone it. But Pete was a good trainer. He taught her how to push herself without hurting herself. She was happy and excited that she had bought her summer gym membership.

❖

Jillian decided to try to get the to gym a minimum of three weeknights, and then possibly one weekend session. She went again the very next day so that her muscles would continue to get used to the exercise. She was a little stiff, so it felt good to work out. She hadn't seen Pete, but she had no idea what his work schedule was. He had been such a nice person. She really did wish that Marty were around to meet him.

She was just about to call a taxi again at the end of her workout when she spied him coming out of the office again. She waved to him, and he waved back, walking over to her.

"How was the workout today?" he asked.

"Good. I didn't want to get stiff, so I thought I'd better get back in the saddle right away," she said, smiling.

He smiled at her in response. "Good idea. You're going home?"

"Yes. And it looks like you just got here."

"Yes, every week we have to do at least one evening shift. That gives everyone some time to be home with their families, if they have one. I usually work two evening shifts a week, one of the drawbacks of not having a family. But it's okay. At least I don't have to get up early on those days, so there are some benefits."

"I know how it is to work different shifts, and I also know that it is appreciated by those who have families if they can see them every once in a while. Good for you for taking two of those evening shifts," Jillian said sincerely.

He looked over to the counter. "It looks like I've got to go, Jillian. My appointment is here. I'll see you soon I hope."

"I'll be back!" she said and walked out the door, calling the taxi to come and get her.

Jillian went back to the gym the next night. When she arrived, Pete was working with a young man on a machine, but smiled at her. He sure did have a fantastic smile, she thought.

They exchanged some greetings between his two sessions, but that was all, until she was ready to leave.

"Can I give you a lift home?" he asked, and then added, "or how about a taco?"

"Oh, so we're trying to keep business good by encouraging the eating of tacos, are we?"

"Oh, you're so on to me. It doesn't have to be tacos. It could be anything you'd like. But there are great tacos at Paco's Tacos, and some of them aren't too bad in the caloric area."

"I'm just giving you a tough time," she said. "Yes and yes, to tacos and a ride home." *Are you sure about this, Jillian?*

"Great, I'll just get my bag," he replied.

Paco's tacos were indeed excellent. Jillian ordered tacos made with tilapia and poblano peppers with a green chile sauce on an organic whole wheat tortilla. They were not only delicious, but the menu had a star that marked them as a healthy choice. She would have to look up a recipe for these. It seemed like something even Mr. Romano might eat.

You're doing it again, Jillian. So many times she found herself thinking about what Mr. Romano might like, wondering what he was doing, wondering if he was okay, and ever since their brief encounter, she sometimes even wondered what he was wearing. The day she saw him, he had been wearing a long-sleeved, navy blue knit V-neck shirt, which accentuated his strong upper body, and blue jeans. It had been months since this encounter had occurred, yet the images still entered her mind from time to time. Most of all, she thought about his eyes, those piercing, brown eyes. She shook her head as if to clear it.

"What was that?" Pete asked, noticing her shaking her head.

Embarrassed, she said, "Oh, nothing. Just thinking about something that happened at work and trying to put it out of my mind," which *was* the truth.

"I hate it when something from work invades my free time. So, the head shake—does it work?"

"Definitely," she said, laughing, although Jillian knew that *wasn't* completely true.

They ate and talked, then Pete drove her home after dinner, as he had been assigned the pre-dawn shift the next morning.

"That was fun," said Jillian, and meant it, after she climbed out of the car.

"Glad you liked it. See you soon," he said and hopped back into his vehicle.

Jillian watched him drive away. He was a sweet guy and so easy to be around. And fun! She wondered if he liked to ride bikes. She decided there was plenty of time to find out—three months minus a week of her gym contract.

❖

June was zooming by, even though work had been a bit disappointing. There had been only generic notes about seasonings in food or small requests to do, or not do, something at the house. There had been no more gifts left for her, but she supposed that after her one word "thanks" for a gift that cost hundreds of dollars, she couldn't blame her employer. Besides, she probably should not be expecting, or even taking, personal gifts from Mr. Romano.

Jillian still left library books she thought he would enjoy each week. She hadn't asked for any comments on them lately, so she wasn't certain if he was reading them or not. She had decided long ago not to check anymore to see if he was reading late at night. It was a silly thing to do.

She did, however, wake up one June morning to a splash in the pool. It had been a clear night with a slight breeze, so she had left her window open, tired of air conditioning. She got out of bed at the sound. She couldn't seem to help it, she had to look. She couldn't see much, though, just some splashing water at the end of the pool when Mr. Romano turned to do another lap.

This is ridiculous. Go back to bed. She climbed back into bed and looked at her smart phone sitting on the nightstand. She didn't really know why, but she grabbed it and typed in his name. There were all the same old crazy stories, and of course, the online encyclopedia entries about his life. One thing caught her eye. His birthday was just around the corner, July 7. She should have remembered that. He would be turning sixty. She would have to think of a way to make the day special without being too intrusive. She had a week to think about how to do just that.

That night, Pete offered to give her another ride home. She was starting to feel guilty, and a little uncomfortable, about the rides.

"I think I should be giving you gas money for all this running around you are doing for me, Pete."

"I think you should buy me a taco instead."

"I was right! You *are* really trying to make me come in more often. I have a three-month unlimited-use membership, Pete, so it won't really benefit your company if I eat too many tacos, you know."

"I know, but it would benefit me. I would get to see you more often," he said, flashing that perfect smile again.

Jillian thought to herself that they were starting to walk the "slippery slope," as her mother would have said. She would have to give a little more clarity to the situation soon, realizing that she would have to begin by coming to some in her own mind first.

They went to Paco's again, and Jillian tried one of their chicken tacos. It, too, was first-rate. But she couldn't concentrate too much the meal, as she was wondering what, and when, to say something to Pete about their—for lack of a better word—"relationship." Just when she was going to bring up the subject, he asked her more about her writing.

Jillian said, "I currently write a blog called 'Where Broken Hearts Go.' It's a place for people with broken hearts to talk it out and get advice, and hopefully learn to deal with heartache in a healthy manner. That's where my nursing background comes in handy. I have known too many people who dealt with heartbreak in ways that were detrimental to their health. I am hoping this blog will help steer people toward making better choices."

While she was explaining her blog, Pete's entire mood shifted. The upbeat guy disappeared, and he became quiet, almost sullen.

Jillian continued, "I just know that healthy choices have helped me in that area—heartbreak, I mean."

"You've had your heart broken?" he asked seriously.

"A couple of times. Majorly." She watched him as he processed that information.

"You seem pretty happy now."

"I am pretty happy now. My parents, good friends, and my faith helped me get better. Maybe not perfect, but much better. And it's been some time now, too, so that's a plus." She was remembering a quote of Rose Kennedy's she once read. *"It has been said, 'time heals all wounds.' I do not agree. The wounds remain. In time, the mind, protecting its sanity, covers them with scar tissue and the pain lessens. But it is never gone."* Jillian thought there was probably some truth to the quote, but thought better of sharing it with someone who might be freshly hurting. She just didn't know enough about Pete, but by the look on his face, there was a story to be told. She didn't want to pry. In time, he would say whatever he needed to say, if anything.

He smiled, although it looked a bit forced. "Do you like to go to the beach?" he asked.

"I do. How about you?"

"I'm a Southern California boy, born and raised. The beach is my backyard. Want to go on Saturday?" He said, looking hopeful.

"Okay, but I will meet you there. Just give me the time and place."

They made their arrangements, and Pete took her home. She told him he didn't have to get the door to the car for her. She hopped out, said goodnight, and waved goodbye. She sure hoped she was doing the right thing by going to the beach with him, but something inside had told her she should accept. Usually, when she got that kind of feeling, things would turn out okay in the end. As she walked back to the cottage, she prayed that she was right.

❖

Friday afternoon was a warm one. It would be the same the next day, perfect for the beach. She was certain that everyone else would have the same idea, and it would be a mob scene.

She was cleaning an upstairs bedroom facing the backyard when she noticed movement near the pool. She had never seen Mr. Romano swimming during that part of the day, but there he was, diving in. She watched for a moment as he swam the length of the pool and noticed something peculiar. He was veering a bit to the left as he swam. He turned to go the other way, and it happened again.

She wondered to herself if his knee problem could cause that to happen. It was a possibility. He really had to have it checked, but it wasn't her place to say anything. She stepped back from the window for fear of being seen. Watching him exercise and thinking of his knee and the problems it seemed to be causing him, she wondered if he would ever try biking again.

Every time she rode her bike down the driveway to the street, she thought of that beautiful, more expensive bike, crumpled and thrown away on the curb along with the helmet. She thought of Mr. Romano bleeding and his anger and frustration over the entire situation. It had been a turning point for him, and not one for the better.

❖

Jillian was completely right about Saturday and the beach. It was a perfect day for it, and everyone else thought so, too.

Pete had gone extra early to stake out a spot. He didn't want to leave his equipment unattended, so he called and gave Jillian directions to his little "camp." There were blankets, towels, beach lounge chairs, an umbrella, and a small cooler. Jillian sat down on one of the blankets.

The first order of business was to put on plenty of sunscreen. Jillian had taken good care of her skin over the years and wanted to keep that going. She had purchased a new swimsuit at the end of last summer, knowing her plans to head west. It was a two-piece, her first one in a long time. They were not as common on mature women in the Midwest, but on the beach that day, every female from eight to eighty was wearing one, so she was glad she had bought it.

Pete looked like a bronzed Adonis, and Jillian saw a sea of heads turn when he stood up to adjust the sun umbrella. He was a walking advertisement for the gym, she thought.

She had brought along a small backpack with a paperback novel, a towel, sunscreen, sunglasses, and a shirt and long pants for later—if there was a later.

After she had finished applying her sunscreen, she and Pete went swimming. The water was just right. They threw around a foam football, diving for it and crashing into the waves. She had to admit that Pete was a really fun person to be around.

They walked back to their chairs and sunbathed, drying off quickly in the strong summer sun. When the sun became too much for her, Jillian retreated to the shade of the umbrella and read for awhile. Pete put in earphones and just zoned out to his favorite tunes for a bit.

Pete's cooler contained fresh fruit and beverages. After the noon rush was over, he headed over to a little stand to get some food.

"This is my favorite," he said, handing her a veggie wrap in a sun-dried tomato tortilla.

Jillian took a bite. "Umm, I think it's my favorite, too. Thank you, it's great." They pulled out some strawberries, grapes, and orange slices, washing the food down with refreshing coconut water.

By four o'clock, they noticed some people packing up, especially those with young children. Toddlers who had missed their naps were whining. They would probably be asleep by the time their parents pulled out of the parking lot. Jillian thought back to the days when she was a mother with a young child. She and Marty had gone to the beach whenever they could in the short summer season of Wisconsin. Sometimes it was just a small patch of sand at one of the abundant smaller lakes. Occasionally they would go to the beach on Lake Michigan, but only when it was really hot and mid-summer. Otherwise one could freeze. The locals referred to the lake as "the big air conditioner." It could be ten or more degrees cooler on the beach than inland, and the water was often too cold for swimming. Instead, she and Marty would build intricate sand castles.

That gave Jillian an idea. She wanted to build a sand castle. The people next to them had gone, so Jillian crawled over a few feet to the vacated spot in the sand and began to dig.

"What are you doing?" Pete asked.

"Making my dream house," she replied.

"I'll get some water," he said, standing up and taking the empty plastic containers from the coconut water and filling them at the edge of the water. He brought them back to Jillian. They worked on the castle for over an hour, complete with a couple of moats surrounding it.

"You need to have more than one moat, you know, just in case invaders get past the first one. At least that is what my dad used to tell me when I was little," Pete said.

Jillian couldn't even imagine Pete as *little*. "Tell me about your family, Pete."

"My dad's a banker. That's why I tried to be one, but my heart wasn't in it. I wanted to do something more physical, like be a builder or pro wrestler."

"A pro wrestler. Really?"

"Yeah, I loved watching that stuff when I was kid. But when I went out for wrestling in high school, I didn't do very well."

"I find that hard to believe with your build," she said.

"I was a late bloomer. I was small and pretty weak in high school, so when I went to college, I went into banking and finance, thinking I would never be strong enough to have a physical job. But then I turned nineteen. I grew six inches in the next year and put on forty pounds. It was pretty crazy. No one knew who I was when I came home from school at the end of my freshman year."

"Wow. Did you have problems with pain during that year?"

"Yeah, it was pretty nasty at times. I had a lot of nights when I could hardly sleep. And I could never get enough to eat either. I'm really glad that year is over. I still have nightmares about it. And of course, it didn't help my grades that first year of college. I made it through, though."

"Where did you go to school?

"UC-Santa Barbara. It was where my dad went. How about you?"

"The University of Wisconsin for my undergrad, then Marquette for my master's. That one took me a while. I was busy working full-time and raising a daughter."

"You have a daughter?" he asked, sounding surprised.

"Yes, I do. A good one."

"No wonder you're so good at making sand castles."

He didn't ask any more questions. He just looked thoughtful as they put the finishing touches on the castle.

"You would have been a good builder, Pete," Jillian said as they sat back and admired their work.

"Thanks."

Then Pete suggested they rent a beach bike for an hour. They decided to strike the camp first and put everything in Pete's car. Jillian put her shorts back on over her swimsuit bottom, and away they went. They made it back to the bike shop just before it closed. They returned their bikes and headed to the car.

"I'm starving. How about you?" Pete asked.

"Are you having another growth spurt, Pete?" Jillian teased.

"Maybe."

"I'm getting pretty hungry myself. Is there somewhere nearby that isn't fancy? I only brought a shirt and jeans."

"I know just the place."

They changed clothes in the public changing area, and Jillian ran a brush through her hair. That was as good as it was going to get.

They drove just a mile or two up the coast, then turned one block east. Pete explained that he was taking her to one of the places where he and the other "locals" liked to eat. It was a tiny seafood place on the corner. It was packed with people, but they found a spot at the bar and were able to order food from there.

The steamers and crab were out of this world. Everything was so fresh. The bread, which their waiter informed them was made on the premises each day, was flavorful and unique. They shared a bottle of chardonnay and talked more about their families, picking up where they had left off on the beach.

Afterward, they walked down to the beach again, leaving the car parked near the restaurant. They planned to watch the sunset, something Jillian hadn't gotten to do at the beach yet and had been on her "to-do list." They settled onto a small stone retaining wall. Other couples were scattered along the wall and other places on the beach. It was definitely a romantic setting as they watched the bright saffron ball sink into the ocean.

Jillian had enjoyed the day tremendously and was happy she had accepted Pete's invitation—that is, until he suddenly turned to her and kissed her.

She pulled back quickly from the kiss, trying not to hurt his feelings but feeling that her usually reliable intuition had been all wrong. She had seriously thought that they could keep this on the "friendship" level, but apparently she was dead wrong.

"I'm sorry. Did I do something wrong?" he asked.

"No, it's... You're a nice guy, Pete."

"Oh, no. It's never a good sign when a woman starts a conversation with 'you're a nice guy.'"

"But it's true. You are a nice guy, Pete."

"No, I'm not," he said a bit gruffly, and the same look from the other night returned to his face.

"Why do you say that?" she asked.

"Because I'm really *not* a nice person. Just ask my former fiancée."

Jillian had felt the other evening at Paco's that there was a story to be told. It was time.

"What happened?" she asked gently.

"I cheated on her, that's what happened. When we were engaged. She was the best thing that ever happened to me in my entire life, and I completely and utterly ruined it."

Jillian just sat quietly and looked expectantly at him, giving him permission to continue if he wanted.

"We met in college—senior year. She went off to work in San Francisco after graduation, and I came back down here. My dad helped me get a good job at a bank in L.A. We were miserable without each other. That's when I knew that I was really in love for the first time. I couldn't get her out of my head, no matter how hard I tried. We started meeting halfway between here and there every chance that we had. We were so in love. That went on for two years, and I couldn't take it anymore. I proposed at the Lone Cypress at Carmel, and amazingly, she said, 'yes.' She interviewed for a job down here and was planning to move here.

"And then *it* happened. It was with one of the girls from high school, whom I had had a crush on forever but who wouldn't give me the time of day back then. I was with some friends, and we ran into each other at a bar. I had too much to drink, and she started talking about what a big mistake she had made passing me up in high school, and if only she had known how hot I was going to get... I just ate it up. She offered me a ride home, and she came on to me, and I didn't stop her. Looking back, I just can't imagine how I could have made such a huge, stupid mistake."

Jillian had known that feeling very well—a couple of times in her lifetime.

"I understand," was all that she said.

"You were talking about how people do destructive things after heartbreak. I did that for a while—lots of drinking, lots of women—after she, Kelly, broke off the engagement. It was *more* stupid on top of stupid. If it hadn't been for the gym, I don't know what I would have done or where I might have ended up. I started working out more and more, and felt better and better. It was the only thing that kept me going—all that exercise."

Pete's words made Jillian's mind pop back to her home and to her employer. *That's why he's always swimming and working out, isn't it? He's trying to feel better, to ease and forget the pain.*

Pete continued, "I was just a member at that time, but I used to help some of the new people who were just starting at the gym, and one of them said I'd make a great personal trainer. It was like a lightbulb switched on. I looked into programs right away. I hated my job with a passion. I saved like crazy for a few months, then quit, cashed in my 401K, and went back to school. My father was furious. Later, the gym hired me as a personal trainer, and then as assistant manager, too. I love it there, although I dream of owning my own gym someday. I even have a name picked out."

"What is it?"

"For Pete's Sake," he said, "and our motto will be, '*For Pete's sake, get in shape!*'"

"I love it."

"You would. You love everything and everybody, don't you?"

"I try, Pete. That's what I think God put us on earth to do, to love each other."

"That's why I wanted to kiss you. I still want to..."

Jillian cut him off. "Pete—first of all, I'm too old for you."

"No you're not, I'm sure you're a bit older..."

"How old are you, Pete?"

"Thirty-three."

"There are kids I used to baby-sit who are now thirty-three."

"No," he said.

"Yes. But age isn't the real issue here. Most importantly, you are still in love with someone else. I can tell." She let that sink in for a moment, then continued, "Is Kelly married now?"

"No...well, not the last that I knew anyway, which was about eighteen months ago. She's still in San Francisco."

"So, what are you doing down here? Have you tried talking to her?"

"She won't talk to me."

"When was the last time you tried?"

"A few years ago."

"I think you should try again. Time helps a lot. It's true, she may never speak to you again, but is she *worth* giving it another try, or even more than one?"

"Yes," he said, quietly.

"Then it's a no-brainer, Pete. True love doesn't grow on trees. It's worth giving it another shot."

"Okay, heart doctor, I will."

His choice of words jolted her. If he only knew her entire story, which all began with wanting to be a heart doctor, which began by simply watching a television program called *O.R.,* which starred some amazing actors, one of whom was her current employer and lived a few hundred feet away from her. What were the chances of that of that happening? She sometimes wondered why and looked at the stars in the sky, like she had her first night in the cottage, searching for an answer. She wondered if she would ever get an answer.

Jillian turned her attention back to Pete. "This has been a special day, Pete. But right now, I'm getting close to crashing. Would you mind taking me home?"

"Sure thing," he said and gave her a hug. "Jillian, we can still be friends, can't we? I need more friends like you."

"Yes, Pete. I need more friends like you, too."

Chapter Thirteen

It was the Fourth of July, and Jillian had the day off. She and Drew were going to Karen and Robert's for a cookout. Karen told them to bring their swimsuits, as the Wilsons had a huge kidney-shaped pool in the backyard. It was a postcard perfect summer day.

The four of them swam and talked and sunbathed. There was a gentle breeze, and palm trees were rustling above them. The scent of blossoming flowers filled the air. It was very relaxing and dream-like.

The guys started the grill. Jillian never could understand why men, who would rarely touch a cooking utensil in the kitchen, were so attracted to grilling food outdoors. Maybe it was the fire thing. Robert was one of those men. He never helped in the kitchen, and even though Karen loved to cook, Jillian could tell that her friend was appreciative of a break. Jillian was also, even though she had left a little extra food for Mr. Romano the evening before, along with a red, white, and blue strawberry and blueberry yogurt parfait, as a special touch for the holiday.

Karen had been ecstatic when Jillian had arrived earlier that afternoon. She had applied, and been accepted, to a very special program at Cal State-Los Angeles. She would earn a bachelor's of education degree in Urban Learning, the only program of its kind in the United States. It would only take her three semesters to finish her undergraduate requirements, then she would do a semester of student teaching. She hoped after that to pursue a master's degree and become a reading and language arts specialist in the schools.

"I just can't imagine what it would be like not to be able to read," Karen had explained about her choice of studies. "I want those kids, and all kids, to be able to read and be able to enter into new worlds, just like we do every month in our book club."

Jillian could tell that Robert was simultaneously proud of Karen and a bit wary of her school plans, which included working with disadvantaged kids in the tough, urban schools of L.A., but he held his tongue. He seemed committed to helping Karen achieve her goals, even if he didn't completely understand them. For the first time since she had met the couple, Jillian saw the love that Robert had for Karen, and she was so happy for her friend.

Jillian laid back on the chaise lounge and closed her eyes. Lately, the feeling she had had a few months before kept creeping back into her heart. It was the feeling that something was missing in her life. She couldn't remember having that feeling until she moved out to California and didn't really understand why it kept resurfacing. She had found a church, made new friends, joined a book club, bought a new bike and used it regularly, and gone out on dates. The only thing on her goal list that hadn't been checked off was buying a guitar. She had decided that that would be her Christmas gift to herself, if she could wait that long.

Maybe it's homesickness. She video-chatted often with her daughter, but she rarely talked to her better friends back in Madison. Maybe she needed to talk to people like her nursing mentor and friend Carol, who was always so wise and probably knew her better than she knew herself. Or Jen or Kate. And then there was Jess.

Kathy J. Jacobson

Yes, she needed to call people and at least touch base. It had been way too long. They all kept in contact via social media, but that wasn't the same as hearing one another's voices, and there were certain things you just couldn't—and shouldn't—express on the Internet.

Robert had grilled some chicken, ribs, and fish to perfection. The fish—which was fresh, of course—was out of this world, served with a sauce of Karen's own concocting. Jillian thought she should bottle it—seriously. Jillian would never tire of the fruits of the ocean, although she did miss sweet corn. They had it in the store, but nothing beat sweet corn fresh from the field, sold out of a roadside stand or the back of a pickup truck. She even had a taste for a bratwurst, more commonly referred to as a "brat," even though she usually only had one or two every summer as they weren't the healthiest of fare.

She was happy that California was a big dairy state, so she didn't have to miss those products—not too many of them anyway. She hadn't seen any fresh cheese curds in the stores or deep-fried ones on the menus at any restaurants. Yes, the more she thought about it, perhaps the problem really *was* homesickness.

After dinner, everyone walked down to a local park where some bands were performing. They enjoyed the music, which concluded just before fireworks. It was a small display, mostly due to the dense population of the area and the dry weather, but everyone seemed to like them. People seemed to "ooh and aah" as the "bombs burst into air," no matter what.

It had been a great day. She was tired and was grateful for a ride home from Drew. He didn't bother to get out of the car when he dropped her off. It appeared that he had given up on trying to kiss her goodnight lately and seemed to accept that they were just friends—most of the time anyway.

Jillian retreated to her cottage, feeling sleepy. All the sunshine had made her tired, so she decided to put her blog post off until the next day. She imagined that most people were busy anyway. Tomorrow she would ask what people had done with their holiday, and she wanted to share the healing she was observing in her friends' relationship with her husband, not revealing any identities or identifiable details, of course.

She brushed her teeth, threw on some sleep shorts and an old T-shirt, and "hit the hay," as her mom used to say. Jillian dreamed about her parents that night. She woke up the next morning remembering bits and pieces of it, but mostly thinking about how happy they had been together. Jillian wondered what that must have felt like—to have a marriage like theirs.

She felt the "something missing" feeling creep back into her heart, so that evening Jillian began calling her old friends back in the Midwest. She talked to Jess first, but Jen and Kate did not answer. She had a nice talk with Jess, but she couldn't tell her all the things that she felt. They were friends, but not that kind of friends.

After playing "phone tag," she and Carol finally connected. They talked for an hour, until Carol had to get ready for work. She was still working at the hospital and still supervising student nurses. She was a very dedicated and special teacher and nurse, and Jillian had always been thankful for her guidance, professionally and personally. Why it had taken her so long to reconnect with Carol was beyond Jillian.

One of the first comments Carol had made to Jillian was that she sounded *different.*

"You've met someone, haven't you?" Carol asked.

"Well, I've met quite a few people, and even dated two different gentlemen." Jillian filled her in with the details of Drew and then the interesting situation with Pete, who was now one of her best friends.

"No, that's not it," Carol replied. "There's something you're not saying. There's someone else, isn't there?"

"No. I don't think so, anyway." Jillian sounded unsure herself and then started to feel a bit defensive. "There's no one else I can think of, Carol. I think it's all these new and exciting things I've been doing. The blog is going really well, by the way, and I've started to outline the book."

"Nice change of subject, Jillian. You were always really good at that, as I remember," Carol noted.

You never could never get away with anything with Carol or Marty. Those two sure "have your number."

"Really, Carol. There's no one else. But I'll let you know if there ever is."

"Okay, if you say so. I'll hold you to that last part." They talked a bit more about the hospital and the new nursing school that was in the process of being built. It would be a great plus for an already exceptional program. Jillian was a bit jealous that she was not there and a part of such exciting times.

Finally, Carol had to go. Jillian put the phone down and walked to the refrigerator, looking for something cold to drink. As she opened the door of the fridge, she noticed her magnet of the *Irises*. Her eyes always went to that white iris, all alone to the side. She still thought her theory about it was realistic, even if Drew didn't think so. She wished she could know what the real story was, but obviously, that couldn't happen. Maybe she should ask someone else about it sometime, maybe on an art blog, or just someone who appreciated the fine arts.

At that moment, her mind flitted to Mr. Romano. He was a fine arts person. She wondered what he would think about it. She doubted she would ever have the occasion to ask him about it, but she suddenly knew what she was going to do with that third postcard she had bought in the Getty Museum shop.

❖

The seventh of July was a Sunday, and Mr. Romano's birthday. It was not a day that Jillian was to be in the main house, so she looked carefully to make certain there was no one in the kitchen and quickly shot into the room. She put a huge cupcake she had made from scratch, with a fat candle on top of it, out on the counter, along with the postcard serving as a birthday card and the magnet as well. She decided she could go back any time to get another one. It was just a token of...a token of... What was it a token of? Anyway, she left a note next to the "gifts" and quietly escaped into the garage, where she hopped onto her bike to pedal to church.

She couldn't concentrate on the service that morning. She was actually wondering if Mr. Romano would be angry that she had been in the house on a Sunday. When she went on bike rides on the weekend, she used a back door that led directly into the garage. She was also wondering if he wasn't going to think that her offerings were some of the cheapest, and most foolish, of all time. She had to *make* herself listen to Pastor Jim, which was rare indeed.

Jillian snapped back into reality in time to hear him talking about how Peter and Andrew, James and John had no idea when they went fishing one day that by the end of the day, they would be fishing in a new way—for people. He said that one never knew what God had in store for any of us, that there were endless possibilities out there, and we just had to listen to God's voice and our own hearts.

"There's someone else, isn't there?" Carol's words echoed in her ears. Like she had with Pete back at Paco's restaurant a few weeks before, she shook her head, trying to rid herself of the voice she didn't want to listen to—and the face she tried even harder to keep out of her mind.

After the service, Pastor Jim asked Jillian if everything was okay. She lied and said yes, that she was just thinking about something that had happened at work. That was becoming her standard answer to her head shake. She certainly hoped that Pastor Jim didn't think she was disagreeing with what he was saying. She did agree with him, but, just as she felt about Carol's words, she didn't really want to hear it.

❖

If Jillian hadn't been in nicer clothes, she would have just gone on biking for the rest of the day rather than going home to change. She was in and out of the cottage as quickly and quietly as she could be, taking a sweater with her for later. She was glad she had taken it, along with some money, as later in the afternoon she rode to a movie theater and watched a film she had wanted to see. She could have gone with Drew or Pete, but she wanted, and needed, to be alone.

The movie improved her mood. Jillian wondered why some people looked down on actors, thinking that what they did was silly and insignificant. She couldn't disagree more. They were storytellers, not just with words but with actions and feelings. It really was an art, and she suddenly admired her employer even more than she had before. What a gift to be able to make people laugh, cry, feel angry, or think about something in a new way. For goodness sake, she had made a decision to go to medical school because of an actor. Talk about powerful stuff!

She got home with about an hour of light to spare. It made her sad to think that they were already losing daylight each day, even if it was only a few minutes. The more daylight, the better. She and Marty had gone to a summer solstice celebration in Aix-en-Provence, on the same trip to France as the stop in St. Remy, where they had learned about Van Gogh and his flower paintings. During the day, many street performers and vendors had filled the streets of the city, celebrating the official start to summer. Stages for bands were being set up for the evening, and police cars were starting to line the streets in anticipation of the large crowds of partiers they would attract. Marty was only twelve, so they left the scene in the late afternoon. Already the "refreshments" were flowing freely as they headed back to their hotel in a smaller, quieter town nearby.

It had been a great way to celebrate the longest day of the year, but at the same time, Jillian remembered even then feeling sad because she didn't want the light to begin its slow but steady disappearance the very next day. Jillian had once told her mom that she thought she was solar-powered. The sunshine was part of the attraction of moving to Los Angeles, and except for the smoggy days, it hadn't let her down.

Jillian sat out on her patio blogging until she found herself sitting in the dark. It was amazing how fast time went by when she was writing. She could look up and find that an hour had passed by when it felt like just a moment. She needed to finish up and get to bed. The next day was a work day. Her four-day weekend had come to an end. It had been very welcomed. It wasn't that she didn't enjoy her work, but everyone needs a break now and then.

❖

There was a note waiting for her on the counter the next morning.

Thank you for the gifts.

Good news. She wasn't in trouble. She walked over to the refrigerator to check on some ingredients for dinner that night. To her surprise, the *Irises* were staring her straight in the eye. Mr. Romano had put the magnet on the refrigerator door where she could see it almost every day. She had mentioned that it was one of her favorite paintings. She smiled at his thoughtfulness, and it felt like he was starting to move in a better direction once again. That made her even happier. Maybe this would be the start of a better year for him, and she said a prayer that it would be.

Chapter Fourteen

It was late September, and Jillian was not sure what had happened to the summer. Her gym contract expired, but she and Pete still got together to talk or do something fun. On their last outing, Pete had taught her—or rather tried to teach her—how to surf. It was a pretty hilarious day, with both of them laughing more than either had in a long time. Jillian laughed so hard she cried and her sides hurt. A bump from the surfboard also had something to do with that!

Pete told her that he had tried calling Kelly, but she would not answer. He sent a card to her last known address and to her place of work, but got no response.

"Pete, I think you need to go up there and see her face-to-face. Tell her you are sorry. Ask for her forgiveness, if nothing else."

"You really think that would help?"

"I know that I would have appreciated apologies from the men who hurt me. Neither one of them even came close to saying they were sorry or asking for forgiveness. I had to learn to forgive them all on my own. It would have been easier if they would have made some gesture in that area."

"How did you do it, Jillian? How could you forgive them?"

"It wasn't easy—I should say, isn't easy. Forgiveness is a process that is still going on, and sometimes I slide back into old feelings. I also know that I will never be as trusting again, but I am working on it."

She told him about going to a seminar in Madison given by Dr. Robert Enright, an educational psychology professor at the University of Wisconsin and head of the International Forgiveness Institute, Inc. He talked about how forgiveness is a choice. Carol had gone with her. They both walked away feeling like new people. They read more of Professor Enright's books, as well as books by Dr. Everett Worthington and Desmond Tutu about the process and power of forgiveness. Jillian wasn't completely free of her past, but she had come a long way from where she had been ten years before.

" I guess I could try asking for her forgiveness. I've said I'm sorry, but I never asked her to forgive me," Pete continued.

"Another thing you need to do, Pete, which may be the toughest thing of all, is to learn to forgive yourself."

Jillian had had a tough time with that one after getting pregnant. It helped once she had Marty and saw the joy her baby brought to her parents' lives, and to hers. Before that, she was beating herself up pretty badly over the poor decision she had made.

"You are right."

"If you can't forgive yourself, I think it makes it even harder for the other person to forgive you in some strange way, just like some say that if you can't love yourself, how can you expect others to love you?"

He looked thoughtful for a moment as he took in Jillian's words.

"One last thing, Pete. Do you think it would make a difference in *your* life if Kelly could at least forgive you, even if nothing else ever came of it?"

"I think it would."

"Go. Now!"

❖

As Jillian got back to work on Monday morning, she thought back on the weekend. It had seemed strange that one could still surf and go to the beach in the "fall." She was beginning to miss some of the aspects of fall that she liked back in the Midwest, like fall colors. She had noticed a slight color change on some of the bougainvillea that covered some buildings, but the trees remained pretty much the same.

She had been told by the locals to go to the Los Angeles County Arboretum in November and she could see some nice fall colors. The other choice was to head up into the Sierra Nevada Mountains. Maybe Drew or Pete would like to go sometime.

One thing Jillian did *not* miss was the cooler weather of fall in Wisconsin. She truly did enjoy the warmth of Southern California. She had adapted to that without a hitch.

Karen had started her bachelor's program and was very busy studying. Jillian helped her go laptop computer shopping and showed Karen how to use many of the features on the computer she bought. The only drawback to Karen going back to school was that she wasn't as free and available as she had been before. Now she had homework to do and papers to write, along with the increased amount of time she spent with her husband. Karen wasn't looking for things to do with her time anymore and had little free time for coffee or lunch.

Jillian didn't miss the studying scene. It was funny how different it was writing a paper for a class—which she did not find fun—compared to her own writing—which was a *joy*. She had recently signed up for a Saturday writing seminar at UCLA, which was happening in a few weeks. She was excited, and she thought it would help her make the next necessary steps to complete her writing goals, which was to have her book in final form by the fall of the next year and then publish it. The thought made her feel giddy, and she hummed to herself as she cleaned.

Jillian heard the phone ring in the other room. Mr. Romano was out with Lucy at the pet store. She heard his nephew's voice on the machine, as she had numerous times throughout the past nine months. It drove her crazy to hear him plead with his uncle to call him.

She walked toward the machine and listened.

"Zio, are you okay? I sure wish you would call us. I have so much to tell you, especially about John Anthony. He's the star quarterback on the team, just like you, and he just auditioned and got the lead role in *Damn Yankees*. They are even writing an article about him in the newspaper. Please, Zio...."

Jillian couldn't stand it anymore and did something she knew was completely wrong, but did it anyway.

She picked up the phone and spoke into it. "Hello," she said.

"Hello, this is Tommy Romano, John's nephew, calling for John. May I speak to him?"

"I'm sorry, he is not in. May I take a message?"

"That's okay. He probably won't respond to it anyway. Who is this?"

Jillian told him that she was his uncle's current house helper.

"Is my uncle okay? We haven't talked in over a year-and-a-half. I'm so worried about him."

Jillian was worried about him, too, but didn't want to alarm Tommy and also didn't want to get caught on the phone. She gave him her cell number and told him to call her after seven p.m. CST, and she would talk to him. He was very appreciative. She, on the other hand, was very afraid. She had asked Tommy if it was okay if she deleted his message with her picking up the phone. He said it was okay and he would call back again and leave another one.

You are on the most slippery of slopes this time, Jillian.

She felt guilty the rest of the day. She did her chores in record time and got out of there as quickly as she could, making certain that she would not cross paths with her employer.

At five p.m. Jillian's time, Tommy called her. She really couldn't tell him much about his uncle, but mentioned the bike accident, the unsteadiness she noticed the one time they met face-to-face, his seemingly worsened limp, and the veering to his left while swimming. Tommy mentioned how concerned he was that his uncle was ill and mentioned that his father had died from Alzheimer's disease. Jillian told him she would call him if she saw anything unusual. She didn't want to mention that social withdrawal was sometimes a sign of certain types of dementia. The poor man had suffered enough.

They exchanged email addresses. "I'm so glad you picked up the phone, Ms. Johnson. At least I know that he's alive. It's been so hard on our family, having him cut us off like he has."

"I'm glad I did, too," Jillian lied. She was petrified, and rightly so.

Chapter Fifteen

Jillian texted Tommy Romano from time to time over the next weeks—just little things to let him know that his uncle was okay. Jillian started to relax, as it appeared that Mr. Romano had no knowledge of her contact with his nephew. That is, until the day Jillian took it one step too far.

Several weeks after their conversation, Tommy had emailed her the link to the article in the *Libertyville Review* about John Anthony. It was called "Eye Black, Greasepaint and Chalk Dust." It described the life of John Anthony—the quarterback, the actor, and the scholar. He was being recruited by a number of Division I football programs, but hadn't decided yet on a school. He had until February to make his final commitment.

The article mentioned how there were not too many young men who had interests in sports and the arts and had a 4.0 grade point average. John Anthony had mentioned to the reporter that he owed that to his family's guidance and support of all his interests, but mostly from the inspiration given to him by his great-uncle, John D. Romano, who had been both a college quarterback, an Emmy Award-winning actor, and was an Academic All-American.

The article also had two photos of the handsome young man with beautiful curls, one in his football uniform throwing a pass, the other on stage as "Joe Boyd" in *Damn Yankees*. His hair was lighter than his great-uncle's had been, but he had the same penetrating brown eyes and knock-out grin that she had seen on Mr. Romano's face on television and in the photo in the library in the house.

Jillian didn't know what possessed her, but she copied the entire article off on her printer. She looked at the article and then looked at the article again. She had an overwhelming desire to give it to Mr. Romano.

She decided that she couldn't do such a thing on a whim. She would pray about it and make a decision later. She knew that, depending on what she decided, it could most likely cost her her employment. This was way beyond being seen by Mr. Romano, petting his cat, or speaking to the man. This would be a major invasion of his personal life.

After days of prayer and deliberation, on Friday of that week, at 4:25 p.m., she left a note for Mr. Romano—along with the newspaper article.

Thought you might like to read this.

❖

The call from Mr. Mack came the very next morning. She knew who it was, and what it was about, even before she looked at her phone. There were no two ways about it, she had broken all kinds of rules and ethical boundaries by doing what she had done. It was completely inappropriate on so many levels, yet she had felt deep down that it was the right thing to do. She had prayed about it and had done it for the sake of Mr. Romano. She only hoped, and would continue to pray, that this would somehow help *him* in the long run, because in no way was it going to help *her*.

Jillian was terminated, effective immediately. The worst thing was that she most likely would not get a good reference from Mr. Mack, even though he had sounded sympathetic on the phone. He wasn't, however, very happy to be back at square one trying to find help for Mr. Romano.

She had one week to vacate the cottage. Whoever would be replacing her would be moving in the following Sunday. Jillian wouldn't even need that amount of time, and she felt that the sooner she got out of there, the better. Except for a few articles of clothing, she still didn't have much more than when she had arrived. The used printer she had acquired cost her twenty dollars, and she could throw it or give it away.

She looked out the window that evening at the sky, tears stinging her eyes. She had known the risks when she left that article, and now she was paying for it. She would be sad to be leaving, she realized. She had come to love this place—and everything about it.

She crawled into bed and pulled up the covers, feeling chilled, even though it wasn't cold in the room. She prayed harder that night than she had in a really long time. She prayed that she hadn't just made another foolish mistake in her life, and that in the end, her actions would be worth it somehow.

Sleep finally came sometime after two a.m. She had messaged Marty, and they set up a video chat for the next evening. She hadn't told anyone, including Marty, what was going on yet. She needed time to process the situation herself before she did that and try to pull herself together.

Jillian woke up later than usual the next morning. She dragged herself to the late church service. She was sorry to have missed Bible study, but under the circumstances, she might not have been able to handle much conversation that morning.

Once she settled into the cushioned pew in the sanctuary, she felt better. She always felt better in church, and this day was no exception. Pastor Jim's sermon was about sacrifice. He had asked people what they would be willing to sacrifice, and for what, or for whom, would they be willing to do it. It was uncanny that he should pose that question right then and there, because she felt like she had "taken one" for the sake of another that day. At least, she hoped it turned out that way.

She must not have looked like her usual self, as more than one person asked her if she was feeling all right that morning. She said, "Yes," but realized she didn't even sound convinced herself.

Drew was out of town on business for the weekend. She felt relieved that he was gone in some ways. She didn't feel like explaining her unemployment situation to him right then, or even worse, having him sound relieved that she was finally not going to be working as a house helper any longer.

She thought that she would most likely call Karen before or after Marty's video call and ask her if she might be able to rent one of her empty bedrooms until she found a new place of her own. She was pretty sure that plan could work, at least temporarily.

Nancy came up to her and invited her to her home for a bowl of homemade soup. Perhaps she sensed that Jillian could use some good old-fashioned comfort food. Soup sounded perfect to her.

Jillian told Nancy that she would be over shortly. Nancy offered her a ride to her home, but Jillian said she would bike over. That way, Nancy wouldn't have to take her back to the church later to get her bike. It wasn't that far, and Jillian felt she could use the biking time to Nancy's house to further compose herself.

Jillian was just unlocking her bike, which was near the church entrance, when she felt her phone vibrate in her pocket. She took it out and saw that it was Mr. Mack again. She was hoping he wasn't moving up her move-out date, just in case things did not work out to go to Karen's.

"Ms. Johnson?" he asked.

"Hello, Mr. Mack. This is Jillian."

"Ms. Johnson. Mr. Romano has reconsidered and does not want to terminate your employment. Are you willing to continue?"

At first she wasn't sure she heard right. She asked him to repeat himself, and he did.

She thought for a moment. Yes, she wanted to stay, but she wondered what was going on. Mr. Mack also went on to say that she could now use the swimming pool on Sundays after the noon hour, sounding like that perk was being used as a bargaining chip of some sort.

Jillian didn't know what came over her at that moment, but she suddenly felt very bold. "I will stay if Mr. Romano tells me to himself," she found herself telling Mr. Mack.

"Ah...I could ask him," he responded, sounding apprehensive and doubtful.

"Please do." *What was getting into her?* She had no idea how she had dared to ask such a thing, but she hopped on her bike with a faint smile on her face. She started pedaling to Nancy's house, realizing that the bowl of homemade chicken soup waiting for her sounded better than ever. *Chicken soup for the crazy person's soul,* Jillian thought to herself.

She returned home about two-thirty that afternoon and went back to the cottage. There on the door was a note, one of the sticky-type notes from Mr. Romano's pad in the kitchen with two simple words printed on it.

Please stay.

Jillian took the note down. It was a good start, but it wasn't going to do it this time. She had no idea what was coming over her, but she knew that if she was going to continue living and working at this house, things were going to have to change. She found herself dialing Mr. Mack again.

Kathy J. Jacobson

"Would you please inform Mr. Romano that he has to tell me verbally, and in person, that he wishes me to continue in his employ? Also, enough of this 'note-only' communication from now on. I am not saying that we need to talk on a regular basis, but if I see him, I would like to be able to say hello. Also, I am tired of having to sneak around the house, walking on eggshells and hoping not to be seen. If you could communicate these things to Mr. Romano and if he is agreeable, I will continue on." She was really pushing it now.

Mr. Mack sighed heavily. "I will see what he says. I will get back to you soon, Ms. Johnson, although I have to say that I am not very hopeful."

Her phone went off about fifteen minutes later. It was Mr. Mack on the other end again.

"I don't really believe it, Ms. Johnson, but Mr. Romano has agreed to your terms and asks you to meet him in the kitchen at five o'clock. He also asked me to expunge any mention of this incident from your employment record."

Now it was Jillian who couldn't believe it.

"Thank you, Mr. Mack. Assuming all goes well at five o'clock, I should be back on the job tomorrow morning. I will call you if there are any changes to that plan."

"Thank you, Ms. Johnson. I cannot tell you how happy I am."

Jillian was thinking the same exact thing.

❖

Jillian entered the darkened kitchen at 4:55 p.m. and turned on a light. It was so quiet in the house that she could hear the clock on the wall ticking, something she never noticed while she worked in the kitchen, which was often. The clock turned to 5:00, and still no Mr. Romano. She was just starting to think that he had changed his mind when she heard footsteps approaching.

He walked through the doorway, holding his cat, Lucy, who was probably there for moral support, Jillian supposed. The moment the cat saw Jillian, she bolted out of Mr. Romano's arms and ran to her, purring and rubbing up against her ankles just as she had the first time they had met.

In her new emboldened state, Jillian reached down and picked up Lucy. The cat purred even louder as Jillian stroked her and talked to her in a low voice. She was glad that she had been faithfully using her new hand cream, which really had made a difference. She and Karen had even gone for manicures together recently, something new for Jillian.

Again, Mr. Romano stared incredulously at the sight, then cleared his throat. Jillian was very patient. She realized that this kind of moment might not have been considered a big deal for most people, but considering where Mr. Romano was at this point in his life, it was a big deal—a very big deal.

"I would like you to stay, Ms. Johnson."

"Jillian."

He considered her response for a moment, then spoke. "I would like you to stay...Jillian."

She liked the sound of his voice saying her name.

"Thank you. I will be staying," she said. Then she walked to where he was standing and handed the cat back to him. During the transfer of the purring ball of fur, their hands lightly grazed one another's.

Jillian felt like she had the time she accidentally ran into the electric fence around the cow pasture. She hoped that he didn't notice anything in her face, but wondered if he had felt anything.

"Good evening, Jillian," he said while petting Lucy.

"Good evening, Mr. Romano," Jillian said and quickly left to go back to her cottage.

She walked at a good clip. As she closed the cottage door behind her, she leaned up against it, as if to barricade it. Her heart was pounding. She couldn't believe all that had just happened. He had actually told her to stay—in person. She had told him to call her Jillian, and he did. Then she thought of their hands touching and the sensation she had experienced. *What was that?* She vacillated between thoughts that she was so glad her hands were much softer than they had been a few months ago to wishing she had never insisted on a face-to-face meeting. As was becoming a common gesture of hers in recent months, she found herself shaking her head, trying to keep these conflicting thoughts at bay.

While she was still wagging her head, her cell went off again. *Now what?* She ran over to her phone, which was sitting on the nightstand. It was Pete. The head shake must have been his cue to call.

"Hey, stranger," she said, trying to sound like she hadn't just experienced the craziest and most confusing weekend in recent times.

"Jillian," was all he said, in a quiet voice.

He sounded like he was on the verge of tears. "Is everything all right, Pete?"

He cleared his throat. "It's more than all right, Jillian." He paused a moment, she thought most likely to compose himself.

"I finally got up enough nerve to go up to San Francisco. I knew that Kelly would probably be at church this morning, so I put on a suit for the first time in years, went to the late service and sat in the back, and just prayed that she would be there and that I would get a chance to say what I came to say. I haven't prayed since I was a kid, Jillian.

"Anyway, I watched for her as the people filed out, and there she was... I thought she was going to faint when she first saw me. Then I was afraid that she would tell me to go away, but she came over to me and just looked at me. We walked outside without saying a word. We went into the churchyard, and I told her that I was so sorry for the way I betrayed her love and her trust, and how sorry I was to have caused her so much pain. I also told her that I was even sorrier for ruining the best thing that had ever happened to me in my life. I said I knew she had moved on with her life, but now I just wanted to ask for her forgiveness so I could move on with mine."

"And?" Jillian asked.

"And she said, 'I forgive you,' and she asked me to walk with her for a bit. We took a walk around the neighborhood. We were both quiet at first, then just started talking about what we were doing these days. When we got back to the church, I walked her to her car. I thought that it was all over, but then right before she got into her car, she told me to call her sometime—soon. And she put her hand on my arm, Jillian. It felt like someone shocked me. I thought I might have a heart attack."

Jillian knew exactly the feeling he was talking about. Again, she shook her head to rid herself of the thought.

"Jillian, I can't thank you enough."

"I don't think I'm the one to thank, Pete."

"Who else would I thank?"

"Well, you know all that praying you were doing in church?"

"Oh, yeah—right. I will."

Pete was so incredibly happy, and Jillian was so happy for him. She was also happy to be back in her cottage, to have a job, and not have to tiptoe around the property every moment of the day and night anymore. Then she remembered something else to be happy about. She now had permission to use the pool on Sundays after the noon hour. It was Sunday. It was after the noon hour. It was dark, but there were always small lights on around the pool. She put on her suit, grabbed a towel from the shelves in the bathroom, and headed for the pool.

Once she jumped in, she understood how Mr. Romano could stand to go swimming so early in the morning, even during the winter months. The water felt like bath water. She saw the pool thermometer, and it registered at eighty-two degrees. Jillian swam

Kathy J. Jacobson

laps until she was afraid she was going to sink from exhaustion, but she had needed to unleash some of the craziness of the day. She climbed out of the pool and dried off, unaware that her movements were being followed by a pair of brown eyes from Mr. Romano's balcony.

She headed into the cottage to take a shower before her talk with her daughter. She couldn't wait to tell Marty about the roller coaster she had just ridden for the past forty-eight hours. Perhaps her daughter could help shed some light on what had just happened.

"Hi, Mom! How's it going today?" her perky daughter asked. It was morning in Senegal, and Marty was a morning person in general, except for those times when she had been up all night working. She had obviously gotten a good night's sleep, as she was on the opposite end of the energy spectrum than her mother.

"Oh, it's *going* all right."

"Spill it, Mom."

Jillian went on to tell Marty all that had transpired, beginning with answering the phone call a few weeks before, Tommy's email about the article on Monday, her decision to leave the article for Mr. Romano on Friday, her getting fired on Saturday, and rehired today right after church today. She told Marty about the note on her door and her subsequent bold demands that Mr. Romano rehire her in person and communicate with her in a more normal fashion going forward.

"And he agreed to all of that?"

"Yes, amazingly he did."

"And he told you in person to stay?"

"Yes, he told me to meet him in the kitchen at five o'clock. He came in and told me he would like me to stay. He, and his cat, Lucy. She's really pretty—you'd like her. She has the softest fur, she purrs loudly like our Sunny used to, and she has bright orange hair—like Lucy—you know, the actress and comedienne. And for whatever reason, this cat, who Mr. Mack once called a 'beast,' actually likes me."

"I don't think she's the only one who likes you, Mom," Marty said.

"What do you mean?" Jillian asked, her daughter's words catching her off her guard.

"You know what I mean," her intuitive daughter said.

So, in her well-practiced way, Jillian changed the subject to what had happened with Pete and Kelly. She would much rather think about that right now. It was a wonderful story to be able to tell, and Jillian couldn't wait to see what would become of them.

After the news about Pete, they switched to the news about Marty's week, complete with the story of an American businessman who had come down with a fever. They were quarantining him until they could get the test results. They didn't think it was Ebola, but wanted to make sure. Marty did mention that he was about thirty, and *adorable*. Now it was her turn to tease her daughter.

They laughed, told each other they loved one another, and signed off for another week. Marty was off to work and Jillian was off to bed. Every muscle in her body ached. It was most likely from all the swimming. She had overdone it, using muscles that she didn't usually use. Even though she was in the best shape she had been in in years, different sports use different muscles. She should have known better. And she was certain that the stress of the day didn't help her body, either.

She took an ibuprofen tablet and practically dove into her opened bed. She said a prayer, thanking God that she still had her home and job. She also prayed for Pete and Kelly. She prayed her usual for Mr. Romano—for whatever God saw that he needed. Marty's voice rang in her ears, *I don't think she's the only one who likes you, Mom.*

She found herself shaking her head once again, but it didn't help this time. She felt terrified. She said one more prayer. *Lord, help.*

Kathy J. Jacobson

Chapter Sixteen

Before Jillian knew it, Christmas was approaching. It was the season of Advent, and she planned to attend the special Wednesday evening Bible studies her pastor was leading during the season. This time she wouldn't have to miss her book club, as the members had decided not to meet during the busy holiday season—a wise decision.

Things at work had improved for Jillian. She didn't see much of Mr. Romano, but occasionally their paths would cross.

One day she was surprised to see him sitting in his chair in the library, reading a book when she came into clean. She looked at her watch to make sure that it wasn't her mistake, but it was indeed the time she was scheduled to clean the room. His reading glasses sat down low on his nose, and he was so intensely riveted to his book that he didn't even see or hear her come to entrance to the room. She just stood in the doorway for a moment, waiting.

Finally, he noticed her and looked at the clock on the wall.

"I'm sorry, the time got away from me," he said, taking off the reading glasses and putting a bookmark in the volume.

"What are you reading?"

"*Catcher in the Rye.*"

"Ah, Holden. One of my daughter's and my favorites. We used to read books aloud together, all the way until she was about sixteen."

"I always wanted a daughter," he said softly.

"You did?"

"What?"

"You said you always wanted a daughter."

"Out loud?" he asked, looking surprised.

"Yes."

"Oh. Well, I'm in your way," he said. He stood up, left the book on the table, and turned off the reading lamp.

"No problem," said Jillian. "Enjoy your afternoon."

"I...I will. Thank you. You, too," he said and quickly headed out the door.

For whatever reason, the conversation, though brief, made Jillian think of Monica Morgan's remarks in her book about her husband, the man for whom she had left Mr. Romano. She mentioned how Ben was everything she ever wanted in a man, and one of the qualities she mentioned was that he was a "family man." She had supposed, when she read that, that Mr. Romano had not wanted children, and that may have led to the breakup of their relationship. But from the sound of his statement just moments before, Jillian guessed that she, and perhaps Monica Morgan, had been wrong. It made her feel sad that he didn't have a daughter, or any children. But it also made her mad, because Mr. Romano *did* have a family. She so wished that he would contact his nephew, Tommy.

Jillian had enjoyed her one phone call with Tommy. And he sounded like he had a great family. Tommy had a wife named Maria, and they had two children. The older child was their son, John Anthony, the one whom the article was written about—the same article that she had left for Mr. Romano and had temporarily caused her termination. John Anthony was named after his great-uncle John and his grandfather, Anthony, Tommy's father and John's brother. Tommy and Maria also had a daughter named Alison, who was in her early teens.

Tommy still tried calling his uncle every week, even though he now had brief updates from Jillian. And it still made Jillian crazy when she would hear Tommy's voice on the answering machine, asking his uncle to call, but she had sworn off answering the phone in the house. She had hoped that the article about John Anthony would make Mr. Romano want to contact them, but obviously that hadn't happened yet.

She did plan to call Tommy again sometime soon. She had some questions for him as Christmas drew closer.

❖

It was nearing the end of December, and it was time for Jillian to cross another goal off her list. She had asked Drew to drive her to a music store, which was supposed to be the best place to get a good guitar for a decent price. She had asked around at church, where there were a number of people who played in a praise band and one man in a rock band as well.

She came home with her new Martin guitar that Saturday afternoon. She played and played, and realized how rusty she had gotten. She also decided she had better knock it off before too long or she would develop blisters on her fingers. It would take some time to build calluses up. *Sure, just when you get your hands all nice, you are going to do this to them!*

She knew, however, that she would be more of a casual player this time. She would help out with some services at church, but she didn't have to do it every week like she had in Tanzania. This church had many guitarists, pianists, organists, cellists, and violinists. She wasn't the only musician in town here.

One thing she really appreciated about the guitar was that it made her sing again. In high school, she had been in choir, Madrigal Singers, and church choir. In college, she had been in one of the choirs at the university and was also in a church choir. These days, she only sang in church on Sundays, although that was better than nothing.

There had been a time in Jillian's past when she could hardly sing a note, especially after the breakup with Scott. In fact, anything in church, for a while, had been extremely difficult. There were some Sundays that she could barely get herself to go. If it hadn't been for Marty, she may have stayed at home that first year after Scott's betrayal of her and the congregation.

But she knew in the long run that the church had been a big factor in her healing process, and she definitely knew that she needed God in her life. Her new congregation in Madison had been exceptional. It was much smaller than the one in Milwaukee, and everyone knew one another and watched out for each other. The congregation had also been big into social justice issues, and that's how she and Marty began their annual Christmas Day tradition of working at a community meal for the indigent and homeless.

Jillian had been thrilled the previous Sunday in church when Pastor Jim mentioned that they were looking for volunteers down at St. Anthony's Catholic Church on Christmas Day for just such a meal. She signed up right away. Drew had been standing near her when she did this. She was getting so much attention from others for signing up that even he signed up. *This will be interesting,* Jillian thought to herself. It would be a good experience for him, though. Who knows? Maybe he would surprise her and enjoy it.

Jillian blogged that night about two things. One was the power of music in the healing process, whether it was playing it, singing it, or just listening to it. Many people had shared their experiences with this, their favorite songs, the instruments they played. One person had joined a community band after his wife died. He had been in it for five years now, and recently started going out with a new member in the flute section.

Kathy J. Jacobson

The other topic was the healing that comes from serving others. Famed psychiatrist Dr. Karl Menninger had proposed that the best way to treat depression was to do something for someone else. When one is depressed, a person is very self-absorbed and self-centered. When one focuses on someone else who needs help, it benefits both the helper and the one being helped. Many of Jillian's blog followers responded that they were going to give it a try this Christmas season, a tough season for those with broken hearts. The responses to the post made Jillian feel good and filled her with a renewed sense of hope as the holidays approached.

Chapter Seventeen

It was only a week until Christmas. Jillian was cleaning in the upstairs hallway when she heard Mr. Romano talking to himself in his suite. He had amazingly left his door to the room wide open, something she had never seen him do before.

"Letter...seven letters...one of Paul's," she heard him say. He was doing a crossword puzzle.

"Epistle," she said loudly, answering instinctively before she had a chance to think about keeping her mouth shut.

She stuck her head through the door to the room.

"'Sorry about that. It just slipped out," she said apologetically.

"Don't do that again, please," he said and went back to the puzzle. He didn't sound angry, just a bit annoyed. Actually, she would have been annoyed, too, if someone yelled out the answer to one the clues when she was doing the crossword.

She started walking down the hall to gather her cleaning supplies. She heard him saying, "Epistle—e-p-i-s-t-l-e." She had to smile as she headed down the stairs to start making dinner.

She and Mr. Romano still didn't have conversations, but she figured everything is relative. A year ago, she never saw the man, except for an occasional glimpse from a distance, and she certainly never talked to him. So, every little step was progress in her book.

Now if she could just get him to decorate—even a little—for Christmas, but there was not one decoration to be found in the house. She did, however, put an artificial tabletop tree on the table between the two chairs in her cottage bedroom and decorated it to the hilt with lights and ornaments. She made certain to leave her blinds open whenever the tree lights were on and she was still up. At least Mr. Romano could look down into the yard and see some decorations, even if he didn't have them in the house.

She had called Tommy the week before. The first thing she told him was that everything was okay with his uncle. She then asked him what Mr. Romano's favorite Christmas foods and desserts were. He told her about the fish stew his family would make on Christmas Eve, but his uncle's favorite of all was his mother's cannoli, her own perfected recipe over the years. Jillian asked if there was any way she could get the recipe. Tommy promised to get it from his wife and send it via email soon. She had received the scanned recipe the previous day and was going to the store that night to get the needed ingredients.

She also asked if Mr. Romano had had any favorite Christmas songs or decorations. Tommy said he thought that his favorite Christmas song was "Ave Maria." He wasn't sure about decorations, but his grandmother used to have a crèche that she put out every year. Everyone used to want to be the person chosen to put the baby Jesus in the manger every Christmas Eve. They would actually draw names to see who got to do it. It was very special. He said the crèche had been lost unfortunately in his father's things, possibly even given away. He described it to her. It was very simple, with Joseph, the Virgin Mary, baby Jesus, two shepherds, and two sheep—no wise men.

Jillian had thought for a couple of days about this information. She had searched her computer for crèche like that, but then thought perhaps that was a bit too much for an employee–to–employer gift. She did want something that would be meaningful to him, however.

She finally decided on a musical snow globe that had the Nativity scene inside, the same "characters" that had been in his family's crèche. Best of all, there were choices of what song it played, and one was "Ave Maria." She ordered it online and had it shipped to her friend Karen's home, as the company would not ship to a post office box. Karen was going to pick her up soon so that they could do some last-minute shopping that evening, and she would bring the snow globe with her. Jillian was going to get a nice gift bag for it that night, once she knew how big the box was for it. Her excitement was growing with each passing minute.

❖

Christmas Eve finally arrived. Jillian got up early in the morning to make the cannoli. She bought double the ingredients in case she had to make a "do-over." She had done a lot of baking over the years, but this one was new territory for Jillian. She looked at it as another adventure. When it was finished, she stood back and looked at it. It certainly looked good, but she had to make sure, so she tried it. She could see how it could rate as a person's favorite. She decorated the cannoli with some green and red sprinkles on the ends, just as it had been specified by Mr. Romano's mother on the scanned copy of her recipe.

Jillian loved making family recipes, and especially those copied down in a person's hand-writing. It made them more personal, and she always felt somehow connected to the person who wrote them. She had all of her mom's old recipes. She had made some of her Christmas cookie recipes the past week and had the same special feeling as when she prepared the cannoli.

She had made gift plates of cookies for Drew and for Karen and Robert. She almost didn't give any to Drew, remembering how he hadn't even touched the Valentine's torte she had baked for him last February and later lied about liking it. But it was Christmas, and she felt like making and giving away cookies. The rest, she would take with her the next day to the Christmas Day meal site.

She wouldn't be seeing Drew that evening, as he was at his parents' home. Apparently they were going to an early church service at his family's church, then having a family dinner at eight o'clock. She had been very happy that he had not invited her to any of this. She knew that he still could not understand her working/living arrangement and career aspiration, and she was even more certain that his parents would think even less of them. He continually asked if she had looked for any nursing positions yet and sometimes showed her ads in the paper or sent her text messages with links to hospital human resources departments.

But Jillian was happy for now. She would begin writing her book after the new year, and once it was published, she would see where life would take her. Until then, she felt good about her situation, especially since the moratorium on being seen and speaking had been lifted in Mr. Romano's house. Every once in a while, Mr. Romano still left a note for her about something very minor, but none in the past three weeks. She thought that was amazing.

So there would be no Drew on Christmas Eve, and she found herself somewhat relieved. He had told her that he would see her down at St. Anthony's the next day to help serve the meal. She was signed up to work most of the day. Drew was coming in for the last serving shift. He had reminded her to be very careful in *that neighborhood*. Yes, Jillian thought, tomorrow was going to be very interesting indeed.

❖

Jillian was planning to go to the eleven p.m. Christmas Eve candlelight service. A taxi would be there at 10:30 p.m. to pick her up.

Jillian posted in blog that evening, wishing everyone a Merry

Christmas or whatever holiday they might be celebrating at this time of the year. She thanked everyone for the gift of sharing their stories and insights throughout the past year, and wished them healing, happy hearts, and good health in the coming year.

After posting, she suddenly felt an urge to play her guitar. The stars outside were brilliant, and it seemed like their light was shining right into her cottage, calling her to come out. It was a gorgeous evening. She still couldn't believe she could be sitting outside playing a guitar on December 24. She was loving it. She sat on a chair next to the shimmering water of the swimming pool and looked up to the sky. "Silent night, holy night, all is calm, all is bright..." she sang. The words fit this night perfectly. She had always loved this song, and it had been written for guitar. After the third verse, she stared at the twinkling sky again and said a prayer of thanks for the reason for the season and for the gift of the past year. It had truly been an adventure she would never forget, no matter what they future might hold.

She patted her guitar, so happy that she had gotten it, and took it back into the cottage. It was time to get ready for church and her gift deliveries.

At 10:15 p.m., she crept into the darkened kitchen. There was just a little nightlight on over the stove. She was just about to put the gift and a little decorated tree she had found while shopping with Karen on the counter when she heard someone coming. It was Mr. Romano.

"Jillian?" Mr. Romano's voice asked.

She had gotten the gift bag and tree to the floor just in time. "Oh, hello—yes—it's just me...ah... I thought I had left something of mine here, but I see that is isn't here. It must be in the cottage, or my purse...too much stuff in it," she said, looking down at the bag she had slung over her shoulder and patting it to emphasize her point.

"Oh. Well, I hope you find what you are looking for."

For whatever reason, his words struck her at that moment. She looked at him, and their eyes locked. She felt like he was peering into her soul, and she had to look away.

"Umm, I was just heading out to church. Would you like to join me?" She could barely believe she just asked him that.

He actually hesitated a moment, but politely declined the offer. She wasn't certain what she would have done with all the things sitting at her feet had he accepted her invitation.

"Well, Merry Christmas then, Mr. Romano."

"John."

Jillian was dumbstruck for a moment, then quietly said, "Merry Christmas...John."

"Merry Christmas, Jillian," he said, and walked out of the kitchen.

It took Jillian a few seconds to recover her senses, but the taxi would be blowing its horn for her if she didn't hurry up, so she snapped back into action. She left the tree and the bag with the snow globe in it on the counter. She put the cannoli in the refrigerator. Then she quickly wrote a note.

Merry Christmas. There is a special dessert for you in the refrigerator. I hope you enjoy it. Also, there is a free meal being served down at St. Anthony's Catholic Church tomorrow. The meal is served from noon to 2 p.m. I am going to be down there working much of the day. You are welcome.

She left the address of the church on another piece of note paper and hustled out of the room to meet her ride.

❖

Jillian returned home at a quarter past midnight. She took one last look out her window at the starry sky before she laid down to sleep. The church service had made her feel so hopeful, peaceful, and thankful. There had been three guitarists serving as musicians that night, and Jillian hoped that next year she would be in good enough playing shape to join them—that is, if she was still around the area by next Christmas. She said her usual prayers and then laid down, cuddling up with a pillow. Her last thought before she drifted off to sleep was to recall the haunting words of Mr. Romano: "I hope you find what you are looking for."

So do I. And she drifted off into a peaceful sleep.

❖

Christmas morning came quickly. Jillian had signed up to be downtown early to help cook and set up. She and Marty loved this way of spending Christmas. Someone had once questioned her about this practice, telling her she should be at home with her family on the holiday. She told the person that God gave her the greatest gift of love at Christmas, so it seemed the least she could do was to give a little piece of that gift to someone else. She and Marty would never have had it any other way. She hoped that Marty had had a good celebration and had found her own way to help someone in Dakar. She would talk to her this evening after she got home and find out.

Down in the large basement at St. Anthony's, they would be serving ham and turkey, mashed potatoes and dressing with gravy, cranberries, sweet potatoes, corn and green beans, dinner rolls and butter, fresh fruit, and apple and pumpkin pie. It was quite the feast. It was also quite the dinner to prepare and clean up.

People started lining up outside the door at eleven a.m. At noon, the servers sang a prayer, and then the rush began. Drew made it just in time to start serving at noon. She was sure he wanted to spend as little time there as possible. He stood next to Jillian and looked for some guidance. She was also pretty sure that outside of a bit of grilling, he had never served a meal to anyone in his life, let alone to three hundred people off the streets of Los Angeles.

Jillian gave Drew serving instructions and told him to tell the people they could come back for more later after everyone was served. Other than that, it wasn't very complicated. Drew couldn't seem to stop staring at some of the people, especially the most dirty and unshaven of the homeless people who were in the mix. She was happy that he came, though, and that he hadn't chickened out at the last minute, which she had considered a distinct possibility in his case.

She never even gave Mr. Romano a thought until about 12:45 p.m. when she noticed him stepping out from the kitchen, which was just a bit to her left and behind her. He had been talking to someone there and then walked over to her.

"Could you use another hand?" he asked.

Jillian was dumbstruck for the second time in the past twenty-four hours. She had thought he might come to eat at the dinner, but she certainly had not expected him to help serve it.

"Anyone here need a break?" she asked.

The woman next to her, Geri, said, "I could use a break."

"Thank you," Jillian said to John. She handed him a ladle, giving him a very quick low-down on the art of stirring and ladling gravy.

So there was Jillian, standing in between Drew and Mr. Romano. She almost felt like she was in some sort of unusual dream. It was an interesting scenario, to say the least.

Mr. Romano got the hang of his new job very quickly. He actually seemed to enjoy it and spoke to many of the people who came through the line as if he knew them. Jillian felt like she was witnessing a miracle happening. He was especially friendly to a young boy of about nine or ten, who was accompanied by a very big, gruff man to whom Jillian took an immediate disliking, not something that happened to her very often.

Things started to slow down about 1:45 p.m. The last hour had zoomed by. When there was a slight break in the action, Drew went back to the kitchen to get more corn, and John stood stirring the gravy so it wouldn't get lumpy. He turned his head slightly toward her and started to speak.

"Thank you for the gift."

"You're welcome."

"And the cannoli...it tasted just like my mother's."

"I'm glad to hear that, since it was her recipe."

He stopped stirring the gravy and looked directly at her. She looked away, knowing that she had just admitted that she had had contact with his family again, and she was relieved to see that someone was coming up for more gravy at that very moment.

Drew returned with a half-filled pot of corn, the last of it for the day. There were just a few more people left to serve in the line, then the workers could eat, leave, or start cleaning up.

Drew turned to her, "Can I give you a ride home, Jillian? Or how about some dinner somewhere?"

"I'm planning to eat here in a minute, Drew, and then help clean up. But thank you anyway."

He took off his apron and said, "Okay, I'll call you later." He couldn't wait to bolt out of the building. But again, she was glad he had come, given it a shot, and stuck out his shift. This world was very foreign to him, and she was glad he had ventured into it.

She figured that Mr. Romano would be heading out any moment as well, but instead he surprised her.

"I've got my car here," Mr. Romano said. "I can give you a ride home when we're all done, if you'd like."

"It will be a while," she said.

"That's okay," he answered.

"Okay," was the best answer she could muster.

They each got a tray and filled their plates with food and went to sit down. Some people ate with the people who had come in for dinner, others sat at a table with the other helpers.

She looked at the table with the little boy and his father, or

Kathy J. Jacobson

whoever the man was with him, and asked if it was okay if they sat with them. Mr. Romano nodded.

The boy's name was Ricardo, but he said he liked to be called Rick. The man next to him told him to shut up and eat. She noticed Mr. Romano tense up beside her, and thought that if he could have, he would have liked to reach across the table and deck the man. Jillian understood the feeling.

They all finished about the same time. As they were heading to where the trays and garbage cans were located, poor little Rick tripped, and his tray went flying. The dishes and silverware clattered loudly on the tile floor of the church basement.

The boy looked humiliated, then terrified. The man with him yelled loudly, "You *stupid* little... Pick it up!"

The boy had tears in his eyes and looked frantic as he gazed upon the mess scattered about the floor. Jillian reached down to help him pick it up and said, "It's okay, it could happen to anyone."

A second later, there was another thunderous crash. They all looked over to see Mr. Romano on the floor, surrounded by the contents of his tray. All Jillian could think about was the day he came home with a crumpled bike after having an accident. She mouthed to him, "Are you all right?"

He gave her a little wink. "See, Rick. It can happen to anyone. Let's clean up our messes."

The boy, amazingly, started smiling, and the three of them cleaned up the floor. The man with him waited impatiently, not bothering to help at all, with a huge scowl on his face. The boy waved to Mr. Romano as he left, being pushed along by the man. Jillian hated to think about what happened to Rick at home if the man was that mean to him in public. She tried to put the thought out of her mind.

She and Mr. Romano helped wash dishes and tables until about 3:45 p.m., then headed to Mr. Romano's vehicle, which was parked in the back church lot.

She climbed quietly into the shiny black Land Rover.

"I haven't been in a Land Rover since we lived in Africa. Of course, it wasn't a fancy one like this one, and all of them over there were white," Jillian said.

"What were you doing in Africa?"

"I was a nurse, part of a mission group in Tanzania. We were there for eight years."

"Was your husband in the medical field, too?"

"I've never been married," Jillian said, suddenly feeling a bit self-conscious.

"Why not?" he asked bluntly.

She thought for a moment about the answer to that question. "I guess I've never fallen in love with the right person."

They were both quiet for a minute or two, both just thinking. Then he asked her another question, "Is Christmas your favorite holiday?"

"I like it, but it comes in second to Easter."

"Easter. Why Easter?" he asked.

"A couple of reasons. One, in the Midwest, where I come from, it means that spring is right around the corner, and I'm usually more than ready for spring by that time. I also love that the days are getting longer. And Easter, well, it's why Christmas happened in the first place. And it's all about new life, new birth, and new chances."

He nodded his head affirmatively. "I've never thought about it that way before."

They were quiet again, but it felt okay—comfortable. It had been quite a day. Before she knew it, they were pulling into the garage. It felt so strange to be with Mr. Romano, in his vehicle, pulling into his garage. Her bike was parked there, but other than going in and out to go on a bike ride or taking out the trash, she had never experienced this before. She had never pulled into the garage—like she was coming home.

They walked into the kitchen, Mr. Romano opening the door for her to walk through first. She started to head toward the door to the backyard, but turned to thank him.

"Thank you so much for coming to the dinner today, and for helping," she said.

"Thank you for inviting me."

"And what you did for that little boy...you should get an Academy Award for that one. I was afraid you were hurt at first."

"Thanks for caring whether I was or not," he said sincerely, his eyes fixed on hers.

Jillian could feel the blood rushing to her face and neck again. She didn't really know what to say next, so she looked at her watch.

"Oh, look at the time. It's 4:45 already. I've got a date..." At the word *date*, Mr. Romano's eyes widened, and he jerked his head a bit in surprise. She continued, "To talk with my daughter at five."

She thought he looked a bit relieved when she said that, and he nodded his head as if to say he understood.

"Okay, then, Merry Christmas," she said, and like she was watching someone else do it, she extended her hand out to his to shake it.

"Merry Christmas, Jillian," he said, taking her hand and shaking it slowly and gently.

They let go of each other's hands, and she scampered out the door and to the cottage. She had a little conversation with herself on the way back. *What are you doing, Jillian?* This time, she asked herself out loud.

She sat down in one of the comfy cream-colored chairs, grabbed her laptop, and dialed her daughter.

Marty took one look at her and asked, "Merry Christmas! What's going on, Mom?"

She told Marty all about the past twenty-four hours, and especially all the events of the day. She told her about standing between Drew and Mr. Romano while serving the dinner. She had been happy that Drew had actually come and helped. She had been very surprised that Mr. Romano showed up and that he was there to help, and how comfortable he was talking with the people who came through the line. And last, she relayed the precious story about Rick dropping the tray and being humiliated, and Mr. Romano dropping his on purpose to make him feel better. She had told Marty that the entire day it seemed like there was a miracle occurring.

"You're right, Mom. It does sound like a miracle happened… maybe even more than one of them." And then she tacked on, "It's nice to know that they still happen."

Chapter Eighteen

Jillian found herself tiptoeing around the house the next few days, no longer because she had to but because for some reason she wanted to avoid running into John—Mr. Romano. *You never should have called him by his first name.*

It was easy enough to pretend to be super busy, but there were other times when she heard him coming down the hall—thanks to her sharp hearing—and she just plain headed in another direction. She couldn't really say why. She just did.

A few days went by, and she went out for a walk after work. A brief, badly needed rain had occurred an hour before, and it was still wet, so she didn't want to take out her bike. All of a sudden, she saw Mr. Romano coming toward her on the street. She had never noticed him going on a walk or seen him when she was out on her bike rides at this time of day, so she felt surprised. She had never considered that she might run into him. She couldn't just turn around and leave, so she just kept walking until they met one another on the street.

"Hi, Jillian," he said, stopping in the street. "May I walk with you?"

"Sure," she said, her heart beginning to pound again, and not from the walking.

They began to walk, both silent at first. There were two boys out in a yard throwing a football. Rarely did Jillian see children outside playing, but then again, most were on their holiday break this week.

Seeing the boy catch the ball and run for a pretend touchdown, she asked, "Are you going to watch the big game on New Year's Day?

"Which game would that be?"

"The bowl game your alma mater is playing against Oregon."

"Oh. I hadn't really thought about it."

"You mean you used to play football for that school, and you have an amazing mini-theater in your house, and you're not going to watch the game?"

"Well, maybe I will. But it's no fun to cheer alone. Are you going to watch the game?"

"I think so. I usually watch many of the bowl games, especially if there are Big Ten teams playing."

"Would you like to watch the game in that amazing mini-theater?" he asked, throwing her own words back at her.

"I...I guess I could do that," Jillian said, a bit stunned by the offer.

"I'll even spring for some pizza. You *do* eat pizza?"

"I do. I love pizza," she said as they walked up the driveway to the house. Jillian stopped at the gate to the backyard.

"What time is the game?"

"One o'clock," she said.

"I'll see you just before one on New Year's Day, then."

"Deal," she said, a term her daughter often used, and she went through the gate as quickly as she could.

Her cell phone buzzed as she entered the cottage. It was Drew. She hadn't seen him since Christmas Day. She thought he might still be recovering from the ordeal of the community meal.

"Jillian, how are you?"

"Good," she said, not being completely truthful.

"Would you join me New Year's Eve? There's a big party at the Hilton, hosted by one my clients. It's going to be great."

Jillian liked big New Year's Eve's parties about as much as one enjoyed a root canal, but she accepted. Drew said he would pick her up at nine o'clock sharp, and she should be ready to have the best time of her life. She highly doubted that was in the realm of possibilities, but she thanked him for the invite. The call ended, and she wondered what on earth she was going to wear. She would have to go shopping the next day. Now she was going to go out and spend money for a party she didn't really want to attend in the first place. Why hadn't she just said no?

❖

Jillian remembered immediately what she didn't like about big parties, especially big parties where she knew only one other person. It was so loud in the ballroom that she could barely hear herself think, let alone talk. There was a twelve-piece orchestra playing loudly in the corner of the room, and people were dancing everywhere. There were tables, and more tables, of food, along with waiters in white coats and black ties, who offered champagne and other drinks from trays as they maneuvered through the hoards of party-goers in the huge hall.

She felt like she was shouting all night as she was introduced to person after person by Drew and then made small talk with them—another one of her least favorite things.

Jillian wondered if she would have any voice left to cheer on the Northwestern football team the next afternoon. Throughout the evening, she had trouble thinking of anything else but her plans for the next afternoon. While she was out shopping two days ago, she had found a purple knit long-sleeved blouse to wear. She could manage wearing that, as long as the team Northwestern was playing was not her beloved Wisconsin Badgers.

It would be fun to watch the game on the large screen. She wondered if she should make some kind of snack, but then again, if Joh...she stopped herself from saying his first name...if Mr. Romano was going to buy pizza, she didn't want to offend him by bringing food. She would just give herself permission to relax and enjoy the time, if relaxing was possible under the circumstances. She felt excited, nervous, and frankly, a little scared. She didn't quite understand what was going on, and wasn't certain that she wanted to understand.

Drew came up to her and dragged her off to meet yet another person he wanted to impress, and then onto the dance floor. At least the music was good, and for a while she would not have to use her voice. They danced to a few faster songs, then the band played something slow. Jillian realized then that she just couldn't do it. She did not want to be in the arms of Drew, so she said she needed to get some air. She felt like the room was closing in on her.

She walked from the ballroom out onto the balcony. It was a cool, but calm evening, and the lights of the city were sparkling below. She did enjoy cities at night. The air felt good after all the dancing, but she thought she shouldn't stay out too long after working up a sweat.

She was so happy to be out of that room, even for a short break. It had seemed stifling to her, in more ways than just the temperature. It was just not her scene. She wasn't interested in impressing other people. She was glad, however, that she could help Drew out. He had been a dependable companion over the past year, but she knew that that was all he was, or ever would be, to her.

Just then he came out looking for her. "Jillian, it's almost midnight, come back inside. They're going to do a countdown."

She reluctantly headed back into the warm room with him, and they went to the dance floor where everyone was packed together. Some people had noisemakers in their hands, others newly filled glasses of champagne to welcome the New Year.

They counted down with everyone, then the percussionist hit a gong at midnight, and the orchestra began playing *Auld Lang Syne*. People were toasting, and many were hugging and kissing each other. Suddenly Drew pulled her to his chest and kissed her. It happened so quickly that she hadn't had a chance to avoid it. She realized afterward that she felt guilty. About what, and why, she wasn't certain. She just knew that kissing Drew wasn't *right*. She also felt that he must have perceived her accepting his invitation to the party as an indication that she had changed her mind about "them." She should have just stayed home.

A half hour later, she told Drew that she wasn't feeling the greatest and wanted to go home, which by this time was quite truthful. She offered to call a taxi so he could stay, but he said that he had a busy day the next day anyway. His dad, his uncle, and he were watching all the big football games with some clients. It seemed that his entire life revolved around his work, and she again wondered if that fact hadn't been a major factor in his divorce. She knew that she wouldn't be happy in such a marriage.

Jillian thought she should have driven on the way home, as Drew had had much more to drink than he usually did. She was very watchful of the traffic on the way to the house and was relieved when they headed up the familiar semi-circle drive. Drew got out of the car and opened her door for her.

She stood up, and again he grabbed and kissed her, like he had earlier, and one other time many months ago in this very spot.

"Drew...don't," she said.

"Why not?"

"We are friends, Drew, and I would like to *stay* friends," Jillian said.

"And friends can't kiss each other?"

"Not like that," she said.

"Okay, okay. I get it," he said, chuckling to himself. "Thanks for coming with me tonight."

"You're welcome. Thank you for inviting me. Goodnight, Drew. Drive safely. Text me when you get home," she said, sincerely concerned about him.

"I will, Jillian. I'll talk to you soon." He must have gotten her message, as he politely got back into his car and waited for her to get the gate open. They gave a quick wave to one another, and then he was gone.

Once in the cottage, she closed the blinds and got ready for bed. She waited for Drew's text, but it didn't happen. After a nearly an hour, she decided to text him. He texted back, "Sorry. 4got." She was a bit perturbed, but at least he was okay. She did care about him, even if only as a friend.

❖

When Jillian woke up, it was a new year. She sat up in her bed, realizing that it was exactly one year ago that she walked into this cottage for the first time. So much had happened in the year. She had accomplished all her goals—well, not completely if she was honest, but close. She had made new friends and had been doing better lately at keeping in touch with the old. She actually enjoyed her work. Just as she had expected, it was busywork and did not take a lot of brain energy, so at the end of day, she still had time and brainpower left to be able to write.

She pulled her laptop off the dresser and sat up in bed writing. She started to write to her followers on her blog. She described the party she had gone to the night before and her thoughts about it. She had mentioned that it "wasn't her cup of tea," but that she had gone as a favor to a friend, so at least that part had made the evening somewhat worthwhile. That got other people talking about things they would, or wouldn't do, for friends, or even someone they loved.

That made her answer back with the story from Christmas Day. Without revealing the who, what, or where, she talked about what Mr. Romano had done after the boy tripped and his tray went crashing to the floor. Everyone thought that was one of the nicest things they had ever heard of—so very kind. Jillian agreed.

After she finished writing and wishing everyone a happy New Year, she went for a bike ride. If she was going to eat pizza this afternoon, she had better get some good exercise. She put on long biking pants and a new bright-colored biking jacket, and headed out.

It was an enjoyable ride. No one seemed to be on the streets, which was very unusual for her area. She rode for an hour and returned home, refreshed and ready for some football. The hot sunflower shower, as she had called it since the day she moved in, felt fantastic after the ride in the cool morning air.

Afterward she had a bowl of cereal with some fresh strawberries on it. She would never tire of fresh California fruit. When she finished, she updated her status on social media and sent New Year's greetings to friends and family, including Tommy Romano. She sure wished that Mr. Romano would contact his nephew, but he was doing some very surprising things lately, so maybe, just maybe, that would be the next good surprise.

Finally, it was time to go to the house to watch the game. She met Mr. Romano outside of the theater room, and they walked in together, tuning to the right station for the game. He was wearing a Northwestern T-shirt that looked like it may have been from his college days. It still fit him perfectly.

A celebrity sang the national anthem, and the game started. She hadn't watched as much football this year as she usually had. She was a Wisconsin fan, but some of the games were not televised in the area, and the same was true with the Packers. But also, as Mr. Romano had mentioned, it isn't as fun to cheer alone.

Mr. Romano was amazed at how much Jillian knew about football. She explained how that happened. "Only child—parents who were big 'Packer Backers.' We all watched the games together. My Dad and I even threw around a ball once in a while. Also, living in Madison for ten years, I usually went to a college game or two each season, and watched all the other games on TV. In college, I went to every home game, but we weren't very good back then, not like the Badger teams of late."

"My mother grew up as a Packer fan," he said, looking like he was in a far-off place. "She spent the first ten years of her life in that area, where her dad worked in a factory, but then he moved the family to Belvidere, Illinois, so he could work in the automobile manufacturing industry. That's where she met my father, they married and settled, and I grew up."

"I've never been into the town, but we used to drive under the Belvidere Oasis every time we drove down to Chicago. I always begged to stop there. I thought it was the neatest thing to get something to eat in a restaurant that stretched high above the road. I would try to count the cars as they zoomed underneath us."

He smiled at her. She loved it when he smiled. She only wished it happened more often.

"It's nice to know someone who has actually heard of Belvidere, Illinois, let alone knows where it is," he said.

Just then, their attention turned back to the game. The Wildcats were in the red zone, preparing to score.

"Okay, Mr. Quarterback, what should they do here?" Jillian asked.

"Throw it to number 17. He's got great hands," Mr. Romano said.

They threw it to number 17, who scored the go-ahead touchdown. Jillian turned to him and said, "Good call!" and put her hand up for a "high-five." He put his hand up to hers. *Number 17 isn't the only one with good hands,* Jillian thought, and that same sensation she had before when their hands had touched occurred again.

Kathy J. Jacobson

She was happy to be saved by the arrival of the pizza. Mr. Romano said it was from his favorite restaurant in L.A., and possibly his favorite restaurant in the United States. He hadn't been to it in a long time, and there wasn't really delivery service to this area. However, he was friends with the owner and had made special arrangements for it to be delivered on that particular day.

Jillian had never tasted pizza like it—ever—in her life, and she had eaten pizza in many places around the world, including Italy.

"This pizza is like the best of all pizzas put together," Jillian remarked.

The comment seemed to please Mr. Romano and produced another one of his smiles. Jillian had to look away.

There was more cheering in the second half, although Jillian thought better of any more "high-fives." The Northwestern Wildcats narrowly defeated the Ducks. It was just how a big bowl game should be, she thought.

She offered to clean up the pizza boxes and glasses, but he told her it was her day off, so it was his turn to clean up. Again, his kindness was making another appearance.

She stood up to go. "I will see you tomorrow then. Thank you for the wonderful pizza and for the game. Nice win," she said.

"Thanks for reminding me about it and joining me, or none of this would have happened."

Jillian smiled and started walking out of the room.

"Would you care to take a walk later?" he asked.

She paused in the doorway. "Sure. How about seven? I'll meet you in the kitchen."

"Deal," he said, using her word from the day before.

Now that made *her* smile. She went back to the cottage while he cleaned up from their little pizza party. Jillian thought she would lay down on her bed for a little bit and set her phone alarm just in case she fell asleep after eating all that pizza, but she had so much adrenaline in her system that there was no way she could sleep.

She thought about the afternoon. It had been a lot of fun. It was a great game, the pizza was outstanding, and the company was...outstanding, too. She had been surprised at how comfortable she had been with Mr. Romano, and seemingly he with her. She had seen so many things in the past weeks that had surprised her about him.

Mr. Romano was a person who noticed things, even things you didn't necessarily want him to notice—like if you needed a diet supplement or hand cream. He was kind—she would never forget him helping at the Christmas dinner, talking to people like he knew them and then dropping that tray...priceless. And he also listened to Jillian when she spoke, even using her own words right back at her. So many times when she was with Drew, she felt like she was talking to a wall. Many times she had to repeat herself, and other times, she thought he heard her but later something would happen that would give evidence to the contrary.

She made a mental list—he's kind, notices things, and listens to me when I speak. Those were some pretty good, and often underrated, attributes in a person. It was great to witness their emergence, or re-emergence. She didn't know which term was more accurate.

Her alarm went off while she was daydreaming. She headed to the bathroom to freshen up, which seemed a bit foolish since she was going for a walk, but she figured the least she could do was brush her teeth and hair.

She arrived at the kitchen first. The clock struck seven, but no Mr. Romano. A few minutes later, she heard footsteps coming slowly into the room. She was just about to make some smart-aleck comment when she looked up at him. He had a very unusual look on his face, one she had never seen before. She also noticed that he had a note in his hand, and he held it out, almost mechanically, as he walked toward her.

"Oh, so we're back to notes again, huh?" she asked kiddingly. He still didn't say anything, and his face remained frozen in the same, strange expression. She looked down at the note, written in shaky handwriting.

call 9-1-1.

Just as she was going to ask what was wrong, he fell to the floor. Jillian, who had been a nurse now for more than twenty-five years, suddenly felt panicked. She felt like a student nurse on her first day on the unit. What was it that Carol had always told them as nursing students? If you panic, take a deep breath and focus on what you have to do and nothing else. She told them that no matter how you feel inside, be like a duck—calm on the outside (above the water) and just keep thinking ahead and moving forward (kicking like crazy under the water.)

She was so grateful that she had brought her cell phone with her. She had almost left it behind, knowing that she wouldn't be walking alone, but had grabbed it out of habit at the last moment. She punched in 9-1-1 as she checked to see if John was breathing. Suddenly he was John, not Mr. Romano anymore. He was breathing. Then she checked his pulse.

She spoke calmly and reassuringly to John, telling him that everything was going to be all right, even though she wasn't sure that was the case, and even though she wanted to scream inside. She was guessing he was having a stroke, but it could be something else. She squeezed his hand and told him she would be right back. She ran to get the throw and pillow from the chair in the library. She put the pillow under his head and covered him with the throw, to help prevent him from going into shock. Now, if she could keep herself from going into it.

The ambulance arrived quickly, even though it seemed like a lifetime to Jillian. Of course, since she was not a relative, they would not let her ride along. They asked her for details of the medical event and what he had done earlier that day. She told them about the football game, eating pizza, and after that, she wasn't certain about the last two hours. She got the name of the hospital from the EMT and called a taxi.

Jillian felt like crying. Somehow it felt like this was all her fault. Maybe he shouldn't have been cheering like that or eating something with high cholesterol like pizza. If she hadn't agreed to watch the game with him, maybe this wouldn't have happened. All these thoughts flooded her mind, and she felt like she might have a stroke herself.

The taxi arrived, and they zoomed off to the hospital. On the way, Jillian called Tommy. He answered on the fifth ring.

"Tommy, it's Jillian Johnson."

He could tell by her voice that something was very wrong. "Is everything all right, Jillian?"

"No..." She had to stop a moment to compose herself before continuing. "They just took your uncle away in an ambulance. It might be a stroke, I'm not sure. I'm going to the hospital now. I think you should come..." Again, she couldn't finish her sentence.

"I'll be on the first flight I can get."

Jillian gave him the name and address of the hospital. Her taxi arrived at the main entrance of the hospital. She paid the driver and hurried from the vehicle.

Please, Lord, let him be all right. He can't...I can't... Jillian couldn't, or wouldn't, let herself finish her thought.

❖

After giving the hospital staff Tommy Romano's contact information and telling them that he was on his way from the Chicago area, Jillian spent most of the next few hours between the emergency room, the hospital's chapel, and a lounge near the ICU where they eventually moved John. She was not allowed to see him, nor would they give her any information about his case. She had tried hanging out in the hallway as long as she could, hoping to overhear something. He was at least alive, she thought, as people went in and out of the room.

Her plan was going reasonably well until a nurse, who made Nurse Ratched from *One Flew Over the Cuckoo's Nest* look like a saint, came along and rudely booted her out of the area. She could understand the person asking her to leave, but there are certain ways to do it and ways not to. She had had to do it herself on occasion, but she would never have spoken to anyone like this woman had, especially not to someone who was obviously upset about a friend who was ill. She had almost made some equally rude remarks back to the woman, but held her tongue. It wouldn't have helped, and it would have brought Jillian down to the woman's level. And perhaps, Jillian thought, the nurse was just reacting to some stress in her own life or something that had happened earlier on her shift, so she refrained.

Jillian's very first stop had been the chapel. She almost thought about calling Pastor Jim, but she wasn't certain he was back yet, as he and his family had taken some time off after Christmas. Maybe she would try him the next day. She just wanted him to pray. She would call Nancy in a bit and have John put on the prayer chain at church.

The chapel was a small, intimate room, and there was no one else in it at the moment. There was a stained-glass window with a dove on it, behind a small altar. There were some chairs and also some kneelers with red, velvet cushions. She knelt on one of them, and bowed her head.

Her mind recalled the entire last year. She had wondered that first night, exactly one year ago, when she found out she was working for John D. Romano, how, and why, God would allow something like that to happen. She had just begun a new and exciting phase in her life and couldn't understand why a part of her past was being thrown into her perfect plans. This afternoon after the game, on the one-year anniversary of her arrival at John's home, she was thinking about how far John had come over this past year, how pleasant a time they had had together, and how much...how much...she had come to care about him over the year. The thought had crossed her mind that perhaps God had this all planned out, but now this.

She hadn't experienced this much emotion, such searing pain, in such a very long time. It was overwhelming. *Get a grip, Jillian.*

She straightened her back, took some deep breaths, and prayed. She prayed that John was not having a stroke, but that no matter what it was, that it would not cause serious or permanent damage, or worse. She prayed for the doctors and nurses, even "Nurse Ratched." She prayed for Tommy as he traveled to be with his uncle, and for the rest of the family who were upset and frightened.

Then she suddenly thought about Lucy. Where was the cat in the house? Did she have food? Jillian went downstairs and hurried to a taxi and went back home quickly. She called Nancy while she rode back to the house, who said she would start praying for John and put him on the prayer chain right away. She offered to help in any way that she could. She would even come over and sit with her if she would like. Jillian said she would get back to her on that offer if and when it was needed. Nancy was certainly a dear and faithful friend.

She would call Karen tomorrow, because right now she wasn't home. She and Robert had left on a holiday get-away and were not returning until the next day.

When Jillian got home, she started calling for Lucy right away. She was in John's bedroom suite and looked very happy to see Jillian. She meowed, and Jillian took her downstairs to the laundry room where her food and water bowls were located. She pet her, and the cat began to purr. Jillian searched around in the laundry room cupboards and found the stash of special food and treats. She fed her and gave her fresh water. She cleaned the litter box in case she didn't get back for a while.

Jillian talked to the cat and told her the situation. She hoped by her tone that she was conveying something that the cat could sense. She closed the doors to any rooms she didn't think the Lucy should go in, and then ran to her cottage to grab a bottle of water, a knitted prayer shawl that used to be her mom's, and her laptop and chargers. The taxi was waiting, but she didn't really care how much it cost. She would put it on her credit card. It was only money.

❖

Once back at the hospital, she settled into the lounge just outside the ICU. She had gotten a text from Tommy that he had boarded a plane, but it would still be hours before he would be there, and that meant it would be hours before Jillian would know what was going on with John. It was pure torture.

She sent a message to Marty. She wished that her daughter were there with her. Jillian was a wreck, and she was not used to being a wreck. She was usually the one helping everyone else. She was always the strong one.

After a few hours, someone walked into the lounge.

"Jillian?" a man's voice asked.

It was Tommy. She had talked to him several times on the phone, so his voice sounded familiar. He had the same eyes and jaw as his uncle, so there was no doubt in her mind who he was.

"Yes, Tommy," she said and stretched out her hand to him. He held it while she stood up. She asked, "Have you seen him? What are they saying? They wouldn't let me in, they wouldn't tell me anything..." she said, getting emotional again.

"I just stopped in his room. He is sleeping right now. They did an MRI. It's a brain tumor, Jillian." Now Tommy was the emotional one. "They will operate first thing in the morning. They said the good news is that it is in a location where they can retrieve it through the nasal passage. Is that for real?"

She nodded her head affirmatively. "It's called EEA—Endoscopic Endonasal Approach."

"Yes, that sounds like what they called it. They won't know if it's malignant until after a biopsy, although they said it appeared benign from what they saw on the MRI." He looked so distraught.

"I know it sounds overwhelming, Tommy, but compared to some of the possibilities, this is a decent one. I am so grateful it is not a stroke. That was my first thought."

"Let's sit down, Jillian. I'm glad you know something about this stuff, because I sure don't."

"It will be okay, Tommy." The old Jillian was coming back, becoming the calming, reassuring nurse again.

"Now that we have the report and it is what it is, I have a question for you, Jillian."

She looked at Tommy expectantly.

"What have you done to my uncle?"

She got a bit teary at that question. "I hope that nothing that happened earlier today brought this on."

"No, Jillian, I'm not accusing you of doing anything wrong—just the opposite. First, on Christmas Day, Zio—sorry, that's 'uncle' in Italian and what I call my Uncle John, always have, always will—called me just as we were sitting down to dinner, to wish us a merry Christmas. If the call wasn't a shock enough in itself, he went on to tell me about some free community dinner in downtown Los Angeles that you and he worked at...really?"

"Really. You should have seen him. He was a natural. He talked to all the people, and not down to them, but like they were his friends." Then Jillian told him the story of Rick dropping his tray and John following suit to make him feel better. "It was so kind..." Her words trailed off as she remembered the scene.

Tommy just shook his head in disbelief and continued, "Then today—or I guess it was yesterday now, Zio called us to say happy

New Year and to talk about the bowl game. He said he had just watched it with you and you had pizza. And then the most incredible thing of all—my son, John Anthony, was near me while I was talking to him. John Anthony idolizes Zio, and I told Zio that he was standing next to me, and Zio said to put my son on the phone.

"Zio told John Anthony how proud he was of him and congratulated him on all of his accomplishments in football, theater, and school. I thought my son was going to cry...and I *did*. I haven't seen Zio like this... Actually, I'm not sure I've *ever* seen him like this... So again, what have you done to my uncle?" Tommy asked sincerely.

Jillian was speechless at hearing that John had called his nephew twice in the last week. She had prayed over and over that John would contact his family again.

"I don't think I can take credit for any of this, Tommy. Your uncle is a good person. He's just been unhappy—and ill, obviously. Hopefully, now that we have some information, maybe there will be an answer for all of this," she said.

"I think *you're* the answer, Jillian."

She could feel herself blushing, and now she was the one shaking her head in disbelief. "But Tommy, your uncle and I...I just work for him. Before Christmas, we hardly said more than a sentence or two to one another, and before that our only communication was through notes. And yesterday—we have never spent time like that with each other before—and probably never will again after how yesterday turned out."

"All I know is how my uncle was before and how he sounded on the phone last week and yesterday, and I don't think it happened all on its own."

Jillian kept shaking her head like she didn't believe Tommy. He put his hand on her arm and said, "We'll discuss this again another time. I'm going to go sit in Zio's room, in case he wakes up. I will come and get you before they take him to surgery."

"I don't think they will let me in there."

"They will if I say you are family," he said and smiled at her. His smile was so much like his uncle's that it took her aback, and his kind words hit her in her heart.

"Thanks, Tommy. If he wakes up, tell him I'm here."

"I will. Now, get some rest."

Jillian said a prayer of thanks that John had not suffered a stroke, and another that everything would turn out all right the next day. Then, utterly exhausted, physically and emotionally, she pulled her mom's cozy prayer shawl around her shoulders and let herself fall asleep.

❖

She was awakened by Tommy's gentle touch on her shoulder. "Come to the room, Jillian."

"What if they don't believe you about me being family?"

"They will let you in. When I told Zio that you were here all last evening and all night and they wouldn't let you in, I thought he was going to have another seizure. They will let you in, or there might be a major incident in the ICU, like a murder."

She smiled as they walked toward the room, running her fingers through her hair in an attempt to comb it. Jillian was sure that she looked like a wreck, but there was absolutely nothing she could do about it.

Jillian had been in thousands of hospital rooms, and seen as many patients, but was always stunned by how different it felt when it was someone you knew and cared about who was in the hospital bed.

John was awake, but looked very tired and drawn. It was nice to see his brown eyes open, though. It was a vast improvement over her last glimpse of him the evening before.

As they walked in, they were followed by the doctor. He explained the procedure he was about to perform. As he described the nasal approach, John had looked to Jillian for reassurance. She nodded her head affirmatively as the doctor continued his explanation. Afterward, the doctor asked if John had any questions.

"How long do I have to stay here?" A common question of patients, especially men.

"It all depends on what we discover as the procedure unfolds, or if there are any complications. The usual time is about five to seven days here at the hospital. There will most likely be some rehabilitation following that, and depending on the results of the biopsy, other treatments may be necessary. We will discuss the options after we have more information."

The doctor left. Tommy kissed his uncle and told him that he loved him, and John said the same to Tommy. Then Tommy said he had to answer his cell phone, since he was expecting an important work call, and he began to leave the room. Jillian didn't hear anything, not even a buzz, so she figured he was making it up, leaving her alone with John.

They watched Tommy walk out the door, and John turned to Jillian. "Thank you for helping me."

"I'm just glad I was there."

"So am I." He started to lift his hand toward Jillian. She took it and gave it a gentle squeeze. "You're going to be all right, John. Okay?"

"Deal," he said.

Just then two nurses came in to take him to surgery. She squeezed his hand once more and then let go.

She stepped into the hallway and went back to the lounge where Tommy was sitting, absolutely exhausted.

"I'm just going to stop in the chapel for a bit, Tommy, and then I'll come right back."

"Thanks, Jillian. I don't want to leave this room until it's over, just in case..."

She put her hand on his shoulder. "It will be all right, Tommy. I feel it, but I'm still going to say another prayer. Are you hungry? I could get something on my way back."

"That would be fantastic," he said, reaching for his wallet.

"Put that away. You just flew two thousand miles to be with your uncle. I can pick up the tab for breakfast. Any requests?"

"Black coffee to drink and anything to eat. It doesn't have to be much."

"Will do."

Jillian went back to the same spot in the chapel as the night before. There was one other person in the room, but he sat way in the back on a chair.

She bowed her head. She prayed again for the surgeon, nurses, and all staff involved, and for the best possible outcome for John. And she prayed for strength and peace for Tommy and his family. And last, she asked God to help her. She had felt so many different, strong emotions in the past twenty-four hours that she was absolutely reeling. She felt so out of control, and it frightened her.

She returned to the lounge with coffee, fresh-squeezed California orange juice, bagels, and fruit for herself and Tommy. They talked about Tommy's family. In addition to John Anthony, who was a senior in high school, there was Alison, who was a freshman in high school, and "fourteen going on thirty" according to her father. He and his wife, Maria, had been married for twenty years, ever since they graduated from college.

His mom had died in a car accident four years before, and it had been ten years since his father, Anthony, died from Alzheimer's disease. His uncle was pretty much all the family he had left.

It was clear from the way that Tommy talked about John—and the fact that his own son was named John Anthony, not the other way around—that he had a special bond with his uncle. They had most likely been closer to one another than Tommy had been with his own father, even before his father died. In many ways, John had been like a father to Tommy, especially after Anthony's death—that is, until John suddenly stopped communicating with him two years ago.

Jillian was remembering all the unanswered phone calls and messages on the machine with Tommy begging John to pick up. And she thought about the time she picked up the phone and got fired and rehired the next day. She was beginning to see that it had been worth it after all. If she hadn't picked up that phone and talked to Tommy, and later left that article for John to read, and if she hadn't gotten fired and hadn't demanded some changes before she returned to work, John never would have begun to make the progress that he had over the past couple of months. It was all starting to come together, and she silently prayed again that there would be plenty of chances for it to continue.

Tommy was saying something. "When you called last night, Jillian, I thought it was all over."

So did she, but she didn't say that. The thought terrified her, and the fact that it terrified her, terrified her even more.

Just as that thought crossed her mind, the surgeon walked into the lounge. She could tell by his face that it had gone well, even before he began to speak. He told them that things went even better than he could have hoped and that the tumor looked benign. He could not verify that, of course, until the lab results returned. He said John should be back in this room in the ICU in an hour to an hour-and-a-half.

Tommy and Jillian hugged each other, and then Tommy called his wife. He was so happy that he was crying. Jillian had to use everything in her power not to join him. They stopped for another cup of coffee and then went to John's room to wait for him.

Jillian was not prepared for what she witnessed when John was wheeled into the room. Not only was John conscious, but he was speaking—normally. She had seen some pretty miraculous things over her twenty-five years in the health care profession, but this one took the prize. Other than a very red, swollen, and slightly stretched-out nostril, which would return to normal after time, one would never know he had just had brain surgery.

The surgeon came in and gave his report to John, explaining that there had been no complications—that in fact, it could not have gone better. He also told him the same thing he had told Jillian and Tommy about waiting for the results of the biopsy, but that from the appearance of the tumor, it did not look like cancer.

The surgeon also asked John if he had had trouble over the past year or so with speech, or memory, loss of balance or dizziness. Jillian could tell by John's expression that the answer was "yes" to many, if not all of the above. John nodded affirmatively. The surgeon went on to say that he would probably feel better than he had in a long time, as soon as he healed from the procedure. He explained that there was a slight chance of seizures. They would monitor him closely for twenty-four to forty-eight hours in the ICU, then move him to a regular hospital room afterward. Lastly, he told John that the next time he had health issues, he should go to the doctor—that's what they are there for. He could have saved himself and others a lot of grief. The surgeon shook John's hand, and John thanked him, then the busy man was on his way.

John looked at Tommy. "I thought I was getting...it. That's why I didn't call you or answer your calls. I couldn't stand the thought of putting you through all that again."

"Zio," Tommy said, with tears in his eyes. "Please don't ever do that again. We're family. We will go through whatever we need to go through, as many times as we have to, together." They hugged each other for a long time.

Suddenly it was as if a light switch went on. No wonder John had been so unhappy. He thought he was getting Alzheimer's disease like his brother. And all those other things that had happened over the year—his bicycle accident, his unsteadiness as he turned, and his veering to the left while swimming—most likely, all of them were related to the tumor. His withdrawal from the world and everyone who cared about him was a symptom of his depression at the thought of dying the same way his brother had died, and also an attempt to spare others he loved pain and suffering. She added another personality attribute on her mental list— puts others before himself. *Perhaps to a fault.*

Jillian watched the two hugging, and she realized how much she wanted to hug John, too. Suddenly, she needed to get out of there. When Tommy stood up from bending over his uncle, she walked closer to the bed and spoke to John.

"I'm so glad you are okay. I'm going to go home and tell Lucy and feed her. I made one run last night and told her what was going on, and that I would be back. She was good then, but I should go and feed her and let her know you are all right," Jillian said smiling, as she talked about the cat as if she was a person. For John, Lucy had been his closest companion for the past two years, so she knew he wouldn't mind her speaking about her in that manner.

"Lucy. I completely forgot about her. Thank you, Jillian," John said.

Jillian turned to Tommy. "Will you be home for dinner this evening?"

"I don't know," he said hesitantly.

"Sure he will," John said. "Tommy, you have to take care of yourself, too. And you'll want to have Jillian make you dinner. She's a good cook."

Jillian almost laughed out loud. This was coming from the man who took a plate of food she had made and threw it, dish and all, into the garbage a year ago.

"Okay, Zio. Jillian, I'll be home for dinner at six. Is that okay?"

"Perfect. I'll have dinner and your room ready for you. I'll see you then. Now, I would suggest you close the blinds and you both get some rest."

"Yes, nurse," they both said at once. John and Tommy Romano were two peas in a pod.

"Lucy," she said to the purring cat. "He's going to be all right." She filled the cat's dish with her special food, gave her fresh water, and sat on the floor to watch her as tears filled her eyes. She wasn't used to feeling such strong emotions. *You need to get some sleep, Jillian. You're a basket case.*

After Lucy was done eating, Jillian slid her back against the wall. She held the cat and petted her, telling her about everything that happened the day before. Jillian needed to hear it all herself. It had been quite the New Year's Day—again. It was two of them in a row where she experienced something shocking, this one besting the previous, in more ways that one.

Jillian took the brush that sat nearby and brushed Lucy's shiny coat. She wanted to keep her looking just the way she always did for when John was able to come home. Again, tears stung her eyes as she thought how happy she was that John was okay and would soon be coming home. For a few hours last night, she wasn't so sure she would ever see him again.

Jillian's cell phone buzzed in her pocket. It was Tommy. Her heart pounded, thinking something bad had happened.

"Tommy," she said, trying not to sound too frightened.

"First of all, everything's okay, Jillian." She breathed a sign of relief. "I hope you weren't sleeping."

"No, I just got done feeding Lucy, and now I'm brushing her and giving her a little loving," Jillian said with great relief in her heart.

"Good. I'm glad you weren't sleeping, and thanks for caring for the cat. The reason I'm calling—a nurse asked if we could bring my uncle some clothing, mostly underclothes, also a robe, pajamas, socks, a set of clothes for when he comes home, and other personal items. They don't have to be here today, but I could bring them with me tomorrow. I know I'm going to be dead when I get home. Would you mind packing a little bag and leaving it in my room? Zio says there should be a duffle bag on a shelf just inside his closet that could be used."

"Sure, I could do that," she said.

"Thanks, Jillian. I'll see you later."

"Bye, Tommy."

Speaking of being "dead," Jillian was dead tired. She couldn't decide if she should sleep first or pack up that bag for Tommy. Then there was the matter of dinner. With Lucy purring on her lap, she decided to call the fresh fish market and pressed their number on her cell phone. They would deliver some fish, along with some baguettes from the bakery next to their shop, at 4:45 p.m. It was one of the benefits of her current living situation to be able to have such luxuries available only a phone call away.

She decided to get the bag packed next. She went into John's room. It felt so different this time. She walked into this room every Friday to clean it, so she didn't understand why it seemed so strange to her today. She looked around the room as she entered. Draped over the back of a chair was his Northwestern T-shirt, the one he had worn for the game. He had changed it after the game was over.

On the nightstand was the snow globe she had given him for Christmas. It had not been there when she had cleaned the room a few days ago.

Jillian felt like an invader as she stepped into his closet. The duffle was indeed there, along with his robe. Jillian grabbed the long-sleeved V-neck shirt she had admired on him, then headed to his chest of drawers. Now she really felt uncomfortable.

She found what appeared to be the closest thing to pajamas that she could see, then was going to put undergarments and socks on the top of everything else. She opened the top drawer. She grabbed some socks first. As she pulled some white undershirts out, something caught her eye in the corner of the drawer. Bright colors—paper notes—a stack of them in the back corner of the drawer.

She moved a pair of socks over, and noticed the familiar handwriting—her very own. It appeared to be pretty much every note she had written to John over the past year. She was stunned.

She moved some other socks over the stack gently and closed the drawer. Her heart was doing flip-flops as she headed down the hallway to the guest room with the duffle bag. She put it on top of the bed and made sure everything in the room and its bathroom was ready for Tommy. She left the door open behind her and headed downstairs.

Jillian felt lightheaded as she walked through the kitchen and went out the back door to her cottage. She couldn't think straight. She couldn't process anything when she was this tired. She had to get some sleep.

Once she entered the cottage, she plugged her phone into the charger, set the alarm for 3:30 p.m., then laid down on the bed. She stared at the ceiling. *Lord, help.* That was her final thought as she fell soundly asleep.

She woke up to her alarm, wondering if it had all been a dream or not. She was still in her clothes from New Year's Day, so she figured it was indeed reality. She took off her clothes, feeling grimy like she used to after doing double shifts at the hospital. She took a long, hot shower, hoping that would help clear the fog in her head, but it didn't. She felt robotic as she got dressed. All she could think about were the discoveries she had made in John's room. She thought about the snow globe by his bed, but most of all, the pile of notes in the drawer—her notes to him.

Jillian was happy that she had busywork to do. She met the delivery truck in the driveway and carried in the fish and bread order. She had salad fixings in the refrigerator, as well as fresh vegetables to steam.

Tommy returned home about five o'clock. If Jillian thought she looked tired, he had her beat by a mile. She prepared the fish right away. She was going to just serve him dinner and let him relax, but he insisted she join him. They talked about John as they ate the delicious fresh fare.

"I think he's going to drive them crazy, Jillian. He has so much energy, and for him to be confined to a bed, it's either going to kill him or whoever is in his path. My guess is that if all goes well tonight, they will move him out of the ICU as soon as possible."

She smiled. She knew John exercised hours every day. A hospital bed would not be a good place for him. "Yes, let's pray that is the case, for everyone's sake," she said.

The food tasted exceptionally good to both of them, relief being a part of the equation.

"Jillian, Zio was right. You're a good cook."

"Tommy, there's not too much to making this simple meal, but thank you. I'm glad you enjoyed it."

"I did, and the company. But I have to tell you, except for a couple of interrupted naps, I've been up over thirty-six hours. I've got to take a shower and get some sleep."

"I understand, Tommy. You go."

"Can I help you clean up?"

"No, please, as your uncle said, you have to take care of yourself, and I'm sure you will be right back at the hospital tomorrow."

"Yes, I will. At least I won't have to take a taxi tomorrow. Zio told me where his keys are, and I'll take the Land Rover."

"Sounds like a much better plan. Good night, Tommy."

"Thank you, Jillian. For everything. See you sometime tomorrow," he said and gave her a little hug on the way out of the room.

What a pleasant man and a good nephew. Jillian cleaned up the dishes and table in the kitchen's breakfast nook where they had eaten. She heard the water turn on upstairs and the shower running briefly, but then the house was silent.

She headed into the laundry room to feed Lucy. The cat knew instinctively what was coming and came running in from another room. Jillian fed her, gave her water, cleaned her litter box, and then brushed her again, as their earlier session had been interrupted. As she ran the brush through Lucy's silky hair, Jillian felt that she was feeling all too comfortable with this situation. Today the house had felt like it was her house. Tommy had felt like he was her family. Lucy felt like she was her cat. She had to stop thinking like that.

She put down the brush and stroked the purring ball of fur. "What am I going to do, Lucy?" Jillian asked.

The cat looked at her like she understood her question, and as if to answer her, Lucy suddenly bolted from her lap and ran away.

That was the answer, Jillian thought. *Run away.*

Chapter Nineteen

The hospital staff did indeed move John to a regular room the following day, and three days later they released him, in record time. The doctor said they would most likely write his case up in a medical journal as it had been so remarkably successful.

A visiting nurse would be coming each day to check on him until they determined that it was no longer necessary. John could lift nothing over ten pounds for first week, then he could increase that amount of weight as time went on. She guessed his exercise room would remain quiet for quite a while. He was to walk each day, gradually increasing the time and distance. Swimming would be okay after the first week, but only if someone else was around, just in case he were to have a seizure or other problem. He could use over-the-counter pain meds if needed for any headaches, which were the most commonly reported repercussions from the procedure.

Tommy had slept about fourteen hours that first night after their dinner together at the house, then he had been right back at his uncle's side until dinner time each evening. He would be going home the day after John came home from the hospital.

Jillian had purposely stayed away from the hospital, saying she had to continue to keep up the house and take care of the cat. She had made a decision over the past few days. As soon as John appeared to be stronger, she would give her two-week notice. She didn't want to do anything too soon and somehow set Mr. Romano back in his recovery.

She and Tommy continued to eat dinner together each night. She enjoyed this man and his kind ways. Lucy sauntered in one evening while they were eating and began purring and rubbing herself against Jillian's ankles. Tommy shook his head in amazement and made the comment that even Lucy was different. At that, Jillian had started to turn red. While the cat was not too nasty around Tommy, he had never seen her do anything like that with anyone but his uncle. *I'm going to miss you, Lucy,* Jillian thought as the cat purred loudly.

❖

John came home, and Jillian tried to go back to her normal work protocol. She did make up some sandwiches and other light meals each night as she prepared dinner so that John would not have to worry about preparing lunches, but otherwise she tried to pretend that things were the same as they had been before John's hospitalization.

Tommy did indeed leave the day after John came home. He was fortunate that he worked at a firm that absolutely adored him and would let him take as much time for his uncle as needed. But then again, they were fortunate to have someone like Tommy working for them. Jillian could understand why they treasured him so much and were so accommodating. Tommy was smart, devoted, had integrity, and was plain and simply a nice guy. She would miss him very much. She would miss everything, and everybody, so very much.

She couldn't help but think that this situation was her own

fault. She was the one who had left Mr. Romano special foods, library books to read, notes... Her mind flew to the notes in his dresser drawer again. Then she had agreed to call him by his first name and bought him a Christmas present, made his own mother's recipe of cannoli, and invited him to the Christmas dinner. She had completely overstepped her boundaries as an employee. What had she been thinking? She had had no business doing any of this. She would have to give her notice soon.

❖

A week later, when it appeared that John was making incredible strides in his recovery, Jillian officially gave her two-week notice to Mr. Mack during her lunch break. She called him first, then sent an official letter of resignation electronically, making certain it was clear that she was *not* leaving because of Mr. Romano or anything he had done. *That's not true and you know it, Jillian.* She said she was moving on to focus on her new career path full-time.

Jillian had saved a lot of money over the past year and the years prior. She had also received a large Christmas bonus, which she intended to return somehow to Mr. Romano. She would start packing up her things that night, but there really weren't too many new things. She had learned in Tanzania that things were not what made for happiness. She had accumulated a few books. She would give them to the homeless shelter, she decided. It would be better than having to look at them...and remember.

She suddenly needed to talk to Karen. She still had some time before she needed to be back at the house. They had spoken very briefly after Karen's return from her trip, but it was when John was in the hospital, and Jillian hadn't been in the mood for long phone conversations at the time.

She punched her number.

"Hi, Karen."

"Jillian, it's so good to hear your voice. How is everything going?

Is your friend out of the hospital?"

"Yes, ah, he's my boss, and yes, he is home and doing incredibly well. So well that I gave my two-week notice today. I am going to devote more time to my writing. I am going to get all my blog notes together and get all of this down before I lose what I want to say."

"Are you sure, Jillian?"

"Oh, yes, I'm sure. I'm ready to write that book."

"No, that's not what I'm asking you if you're sure about. The way you sounded when you talked before...well... Mr. Romano sounded a little more important to you than just being your boss."

Jillian wasn't sure how to respond to this, so she changed the subject. "Well, one of the reasons I was calling you, Karen, was to ask this. Could I rent out one of your rooms until I find a place to live?"

"Of course you can stay here, but you're not paying any rent, Jillian. After what you did for me, there's no way I would ever take your money."

"I don't know of anything special I've done for you, Karen, but I'd appreciate it if I have a place to land for a while." *Why are people always telling me that I've done something special for them?*

They talked about Karen and Robert's recent cruise. Karen said she had felt like they were on their honeymoon. It was a very special and important time away for her and Robert, who had taken his real first vacation in five years.

Currently Karen was on break from classes, but would be starting back soon. She would take classes this summer, too, then do student teaching in the fall. If all went well, she would have her bachelor's degree in December and start her master's classes the next semester. She was so happy and so excited.

"If I hadn't taken the risk, Jillian, none of this happiness would have happened."

"Yes, right. Well, I am so happy for you, Karen. Listen, I've got to go. I'll talk to you later." She ended the call. *If I hadn't taken the risk, none of this happiness would have happened.* Jillian thought about that. The only time Jillian had taken risks, she had ended up hurt. She couldn't go through that again.

❖

Jillian was dreading her next encounter with Mr. Romano. Would he be angry? Sad? Relieved? All of the above?

She tried to avoid him that afternoon. It had been pet store day. John had just gotten permission to drive again that very morning, so he had left later than usual, but was thrilled to get out of the house again. The Land Rover was still gone when she had come back from lunch, and when she heard it pull in, she made certain to be in a different part of the house cleaning.

Later in the afternoon, she heard the phone ring in the library and John answer it. His voice had started out strong and upbeat, but then it turned softer and serious. The walls were closing in on Jillian. She had to get some air, and quick. She walked through the garage and started down the driveway. She wished that she could just keep walking and never come back.

She returned a short time later, realizing she had to get dinner going. She tried to focus on what she was doing, but her mind was far away. Jillian, who had such keen hearing, was so absorbed in thought that she didn't even hear Mr. Romano as he entered the kitchen.

She was startled when she finally noticed him. *Hold yourself together, Jillian.*

"You're leaving," he said. It sounded like half-statement and half-question at the same time.

Jillian had rehearsed what she would say when this moment came, but the words were stuck in her throat. When she finally did begin to speak, all she heard was "blah, blah, blah, blah, blah...." She certainly hoped that she sounded more convincing to Mr. Romano, but she doubted it. She couldn't even meet his eyes.

"Have I done something to upset you?" he asked.

His words, and the sadness in his voice, were crushing her heart.

"No, of course not. I wrote a letter to Mr. Mack saying that it was not anything that you did or didn't do. It explains everything." *Except that you have made me feel again for the first time in twelve years.*

"Well, then, I guess you have made up your mind," he said.

Again, his words sounded like both a statement and a question. Jillian could not answer him. She couldn't speak, so she just nodded her head. Mr. Romano looked like he wanted to say something else, but she just kept mindlessly tossing a salad she was making. He appeared to give up, and Jillian watched him walk slowly out of the room, his limp more pronounced than it had been in months.

Jillian felt like the lowest of the lowest creature on earth. She finished making the salad, added grilled chicken to it, and put it in the refrigerator. She had made some dressing earlier in the day, so everything was ready. She couldn't get out of the house fast enough, and dashed back to the cottage, feeling like she might be sick.

She went straight through the cottage and out the sliding door to her little patio. She sat down on a chair and put her head between her legs for a minute, then sat back up and took some deep breaths. Hot, burning tears were trying to force themselves out, and they eventually won the day. She sat and sobbed until she couldn't cry anymore. It had been years since she had cried like that. *If you're making such a good decision, why do you feel so awful?*

She couldn't cry anymore, so she went inside and took a hot shower. She checked her eyes in the mirror and dialed Marty. Amazingly, she was online and answered. The first thing Marty asked when she saw her mom was, "What's wrong?"

Will I ever be able to hide anything from my girl? Jillian explained her decision to Marty, using the same rehearsed speech she had given John—Mr. Romano. She never should have started calling him John, she thought again. That's when all "this" began, whatever "this" was.

They talked awhile about her decision, where she would go, and what she would do. Marty was relieved that Karen would let Jillian stay at her home. Jillian said she also was looking into an efficiency apartment closer to downtown next week, and into a room that was for rent in a house in another neighborhood.

Jillian's blog had been doing well, although her posts since New Year's Day had been more sporadic. She had more followers than ever, and many said they were looking forward to her book whenever it came out. That was encouraging, at least.

She had briefly considered returning to Madison, but she realized that Los Angeles had become her home. She had friends, a church, a book club, and soon she would have a new place to reside. She thought she might see about licensure for nursing, too. It wouldn't hurt to pick up some shifts here and there, if nothing more.

Marty listened intently to her Mom go through her litany. Then Jillian tried to change the subject, but her daughter wasn't buying it.

"What are you afraid of, Mom?"

"Nothing," Jillian replied.

"Try convincing yourself of that. Mom, you have seemed really happy this past year. It's okay to be happy, you know."

"Yes, well, " she said, her usual answer when she was getting ready to shut down. She told Marty that she was really tired and was going to take a little rest. It wasn't completely a lie—she felt utterly depleted. Between the conversation with Mr. Romano and her cloudburst of crying, she was completely spent. She said goodbye to her daughter, who was just beginning her day.

Jillian climbed under the covers, exhausted, but sleep would not come. Marty's question kept running through her head, along with her answer of "nothing." She knew it was *something,* but couldn't, or wouldn't, let herself acknowledge the answer.

While she was lying there, her cell went off. It was Pete. She hadn't talked to him in way too long. She was happy for a good diversion.

"Pete! How *are* you?"

"Jillian—I'll tell you how I am. I am wonderful—no, I'm more than wonderful. I am an engaged man, Jillian! Our wedding is back on!"

"Pete, that is fantastic news," Jillian said, and meant it.

"I wasted all these years because I was too afraid to talk to her again or see her, until you told me to go up there. We owe everything to you, Jillian,"

Here we go, again. "Pete, it's not me. God, yes, but not me."

"I'm just so happy. We are going to get married on March 1 in San Francisco. You'll be there, won't you?"

"I'll put it in my calendar right now, Pete. Congratulations, to both you and Kelly."

The call ended. Jillian was so happy for Pete, but felt emptier than she had ever felt in her entire life.

She decided to post in her blog when her cell went off again. She stared at Tommy's name on the caller ID, and for a moment, she considered not answering, but that would only prolong the inevitable.

"Hi, Tommy," she said quietly.

"Jillian," he said gently, then paused. "Is it true?"

"Yes," was all she could say.

"I didn't want to believe it when Zio called me an hour ago. "Why?"

She tried to sound nonchalant and convincing, "It's time for me to move on, to concentrate on my writing."

"Are you sure that's it?"

"Yes, as I told your uncle, he didn't do anything wrong, it's just time."

"But you seemed so happy, Jillian." It was the same thing Marty had said earlier that evening. Then in a quiet tone, Tommy continued, "And Zio...was so happy."

"Yes, well," she said again, using her standard shutting-down response.

Then came the clincher, "Jillian, what are you afraid of?"

"Nothing," she lied.

"I'm sorry," Tommy said, "I had no right to ask you that. I just wish that this wasn't for real. Zio is going to miss you. I'm going to miss you."

"Thank you, Tommy," Jillian said, tears clouding her eyes again. She was surprised there were any left in her body. "I'll miss you, too, but maybe we could keep in touch."

"Yes, maybe," he replied, but they both knew that it would never be the same, even if they emailed or called each other occasionally. "Well, good night, Jillian. Thanks for everything that you did for my uncle this past year. You brought him back from the dead."

"I didn't do anything," she said. *She wished people would stop saying things like this.*

"No, Jillian, you did *everything*. Good luck, and God bless you."

"Thank you. God bless you and your family, too, Tommy."

She put down her phone and sobbed into her pillow until she finally fell asleep.

❖

The following days leading up to her departure were excruciating. She found herself going through the motions of her work and trying to avoid Mr. Romano, and even Lucy. She began leaving notes for Mr. Romano instead of talking to him, and in general went into an avoidance mode.

At night, she began deep-cleaning her cottage. "Leave it better than you found it," was her family's motto when they used to go camping. She had been "camping" in this wonderful spot for the past year and a few weeks. She wanted it to be as wonderful for the next helper as it had been for her. She had given away her books, and Robert had come over after work one evening and gotten her bike. She could live without it for a few days.

At church that Sunday, she asked Pastor Jim if she could store her guitar in the choir room for the time being, and told him of her new plans. He said she could keep it there as long as she liked, especially if she would play it for worship sometime, he tacked on. He was a bit surprised by her decision, however. He said the same thing that Marty and Tommy had said, "You seemed so happy." To which she responded with her usual, "Yes, well."

Chapter Twenty

The day before her intended departure, Jillian made Mr. Romano's favorite meal and dessert and left them in the refrigerator. She also left a long note, thanking him for everything and telling him that a taxi would be picking her up at five the next day, after she was finished with work. She said she hoped to see him to say goodbye, which was another lie.

Once she got back to the cottage, she decided to write in her blog. She knew she wouldn't feel like it the following night at Karen's, nor would it be polite to hole up in her room writing the very first night she was there. It would be just her and Karen, as Robert was on a short business trip. The taxi would take her to Karen's when her workday was over.

Jillian wrote about her current situation in her blog and was stunned by some of the responses. Her readers were "calling her on the carpet," as Jillian's mom would have said. One reader said it sounded like she was avoiding something. Another one said it sounded like she was running away. And the real kicker was "What are you afraid of?" She tried to make it sound like they had it all wrong, but she knew deep inside, they had it all right.

That final night in the cottage she could not sleep. About two a.m., she went out and sat on her patio and looked to the sky. And before she knew it, she was down on her knees. Even thought it seemed a little late for it, she prayed that somehow she would know whether or not she was making the right decision.

She didn't know how long she stayed in that position, but it was long enough for her to eventually curl up in a ball and fall asleep on the bricks. She awakened to the sound of the sprinkler system going on at the next door neighbor's house, and being chilled to the bone. She went back inside and lay awake until dawn.

Jillian took one last shower under the "sunflower," then cleaned it up after herself. She would take the towel and washcloth into the house and put them in the laundry room. She had everything packed up and next to the door for her departure at the end of the day. She couldn't believe it was really happening.

She quietly entered the kitchen. It was dark and quiet. In fact, the entire house was dark and quiet. At first, she was frightened. She thought something had happened to Mr. Romano, so she went from room to room to make certain he was okay. There was no sign of him, or Lucy, on the premises.

Her note was gone from the counter, but there was none left in response. She didn't really blame him. What was there to say? She made a dinner and put it into the refrigerator. She did the few chores she had left throughout the day.

In the afternoon, since Mr. Romano had not returned, she decided to make a final tour of the property. She started in the backyard. She loved the orange trees and the roses. There was an olive tree, too, which had always reminded her of the Holy Land. It was a beautiful yard, and she would miss walking through it each day. She picked an orange and took it with her for later.

The pool was sparkling in the afternoon sun. She had enjoyed swimming in the pool, but mostly she thought about the splash Mr. Romano made when he dove into the water early in the mornings. She thought about that very first day when she had seen him standing in the light of early dawn. She touched the steel railing. Mr. Romano used this pool nearly every day. He touched this railing nearly every day. *Stop.* She had to put these thoughts out of her mind.

She went back into the house. The library was one of her favorite rooms. Mr. Romano's reading glasses and his latest book sat on the table. There was the throw and the pillow she had used to keep him warm and comfortable the day he had collapsed on the floor of the kitchen. She straightened them, even though they didn't need it, and moved on.

She went to the guest room where Tommy had stayed while he was there. He was such a good man—so kind, and so caring. *Just like his uncle. Stop it, Jillian.*

She entered John's room. It was messier than she was used to seeing it. The snow globe was no longer on the nightstand and it made her feel sad, and there was no school T-shirt over the back of the chair. She wondered if the notes were still in his drawer, but she didn't dare look. The room smelled of John's—Mr. Romano's—scent. She had to leave.

Jillian went down to the laundry room. There were Lucy's bowls with her name on them, the litter box, and her brush. She would miss the "beast," as Mr. Mack had called her.

She entered the theater room, remembering their pizza party and watching the football game on New Year's Day. It had been a special afternoon.

Finally, she went to the kitchen. Most of her memories were in this very room. She thought about the man who put the dish of food, plate and all, into the garbage that first week she worked there. He wasn't that man anymore, and Tommy's words came to her mind: *You brought my uncle back from the dead.* And a voice inside Jillian said, *No, Tommy, he brought me back from the dead.*

She thought about all of their notes back and forth, and the ones of hers that he kept, or had kept, in his drawer.

She thought about him sitting at the counter late at night reading books. This room was also where she had met Lucy—and Mr. Romano—for the first time. She remembered the look on his face when he saw her holding his purring cat, who supposedly hated everyone but him, and the way his eyes had penetrated hers.

Jillian remembered Christmas evening, when they stood there talking after working at the community meal. She remembered their handshake before she went back to the cottage to call Marty, and as she learned later, he had gone to call Tommy for the first time in two years.

And she thought of him crumbling to the floor on New Year's Day, and how afraid she was she would lose... She heard that recurring question again in her mind, *What are you afraid of?* That had been the question of the week in her life, asked of her by more than one person. *I can't lose another person who I...who I...*

And she remembered the day in this very room when Mr. Romano had told her to stay, at her bold request to hear it from his own lips. Suddenly, she wished he were there again, telling her to stay—one last time. But he must not want to, because he was nowhere to be found. He hadn't been home all day. It was her own fault, she knew. It was too late now anyway. The way she had treated him the past two weeks, she didn't deserve the time of day from him, let alone to be asked to stay.

Jillian realized at that moment, that she was perhaps making the *biggest* mistake of her life to date, and she had made some real doozies in her time. She thought about her prayer the night before—that God would let her know if she was making the right decision or not—and now she was pretty the answer was "no." But there seemed to be no way out at this point.

She sadly left the kitchen, making certain the door was locked behind her. She walked back to the cottage and checked every room one last time. Then she picked up her suitcases and laptop case, and slowly trudged to the driveway. The cases felt like they were filled with cement. She sincerely hoped that the taxi would be on time. She had to get away from this place as soon as possible.

Jillian stood in the driveway, feeling like a fraud. The entire past year, she had helped others like Karen and Pete, move on with, and repair, their relationships. For the entire past year, she had written a blog that encouraged and gave advice to the brokenhearted, about how to handle heartbreak in healthy ways. She sure could dish it out, but she couldn't take it. *Too bad you can't follow your own advice, Jillian.* She wondered if she could ever write another word, considering the way she felt at that moment.

Tears were gathering behind her eyes, when all of a sudden she caught a glimpse of a blur of orange coming from the front door of the house and heading right toward her.

"Lucy!" she said, picking up the cat. "What are you doing out here, honey? Are you running away, too?" she whispered to the purring feline.

Then she saw John coming from the house. He was probably looking for his escaped cat, but as he came closer, she noticed that he had a notepad and a pen in his hands.

He stopped a few feet away from her, never taking his eyes off hers. She wanted to look away, but couldn't seem to break free of his gaze.

He looked down at the notepad and wrote something. He detached the sheet from the pad and handed it to Jillian. She put Lucy down, and the cat encircled her ankles, purring loudly. Jillian took the note from John and looked at it. There were just two words printed on it.

Please stay.

She put her hand out to John, palm side up, waiting for the notepad and pen. He handed them to her and she wrote one word.

Why?

He extended his hand for the notepad and pen looked at it thoughtfully for a moment, then wrote again.

She read the note and smiled at his words, extending her hand for the notepad one last time. She wrote one more word to him.

NOTED!

Just then the taxi pulled up. Jillian walked over to the driver's window and indicated that he should roll it down. John couldn't hear what she said to the cabbie, but he watched her hand him some cash. Then the driver drove off in a huff.

Jillian walked back over to John, Lucy, and her suitcases. She lifted up the handle of one of the suitcases and gave it to John to pull. She put the laptop case over her shoulder and started pulling the other case with her left hand in the direction of the house. She stopped for a moment, to let John catch up to her. John stopped at her side and put his free hand into hers.

Together, John and Jillian headed toward the front door of the Storybook home, the place God had led her, the place she was supposed to be, she now knew. Jillian smiled as she realized that for once in her life, she was actually going to take her own advice, and that there was a distinct possibility she might just achieve all the goals on her list—in their entirety. She was ready to move on. She was ready to take a risk. Jillian was *finally* ready to give love another chance.

The End

Questions for Discussion

1. Jillian is making significant changes in her life all at once. What are they? Do you think she is wise to make them simultaneously? Why, or why not?

2. What is she risking by making these changes? What would she be risking if she didn't make these changes?

3. Have you ever taken similar risks? What was the outcome? Are there risks you didn't make that you wish you had?

4. Jillian's daughter, Marty, is living and working on the other side of the world. Have you ever been separated from a loved one in such a way?

5. As a nineteen-year-old nursing student, Jillian was very influenced by a strong female character on a television show. It led her to change her course of study, which in turn, led her to the scene of a "life-altering" decision. Were you ever inspired by a person, real or fictional, in such a way?

6. Jillian's life-altering decision resulted in her becoming an unmarried mother. While it definitely presented challenges for her, i.e., not fitting in with co-workers who were either single or married with children, her daughter turned out to be one of the most wonderful blessings of her life. Have you, or someone you know, had a similar experience where good came out of a questionable decision?

7. Jillian made a list of goals/promises to herself upon embarking on her adventure. Have you ever made a similar list? Was is helpful? If yes, how so?

8. After living in the Midwest all but a few months of her life (with the exception of her missionary work in Africa) Jillian moved to a place where she knew no one. In her new place, she is working for a person who does not want to know her and where she has

no co-workers as she did when she was a nurse. She has to make a conscious effort to meet new people. Her first new friends were found at church, and later a book club. If you were moving to a new place, how would you go about finding new companions?

9. How would you feel if you were excited to be on a new adventure, and then had a "piece of your past" thrown into your present, as Jillian experienced when she found out that her employer was John D. Romano?

10. John was very unhappy and lonely, pulling away from what he loves—acting and his nephew, Tommy and his family, mostly because he feared he had a disease that claimed the life of his brother. How do you react when you are fearful? How could John have avoided these fears? What do you believe was most helpful in helping him become a healthier, happier person, even before he knew his actual diagnosis?

11. One of the things Jillian does every night is pray—for her daughter, friends near and far, for her to be a "helper" to someone, and for Mr. Romano, even when his behaviors are annoying or unkind. Have you ever prayed for someone you don't know very well, or was even unkind to you, but you knew was suffering in some way? Do you think it helped the person you prayed for? Did it help you?

12. Many of Jillian's actions inspire people whom she meets, even if she doesn't intentionally try to do so. For instance, Karen from the book club is impressed by Jillian's move to California and major career change. It prompts her to take an online course, then eventually to go back to college and finish her degree. She is also inspired by Jillian's comments about how her mother used to prompt her father to stop working so much and be more involved with his family. Karen uses some of Jillian's mom's "tactics" with her own workaholic husband, with favorable results. Have you ever been inspired by someone in similar ways? Have you ever in-

spired someone else with your actions/stories, possibly without even intending to?

13. One of Jillian's blog followers mentioned that sometimes people date others they know are "safe," in order to avoid the risks involved in really loving someone. What are the risks of loving? What are the risks of not loving?

14. Jillian's friend, Pete, made a huge mistake when he was a young, engaged man. Jillian suggests that he not only apologize, but ask for forgiveness, for his former fiancée's sake, and for his own. Would you be able to forgive Pete? What would be the benefits of forgiving—including forgiving oneself?

15. It would have been easy for Jillian to enter a very serious relationship, possibly marriage, with Drew. Drew had a respectable career, money, good looks, and even went to her church. Do you think Jillian should have been more practical and just given into a relationship with him? Why or why not?

16. When John has a "medical event," Jillian temporarily loses her usual nurse's calm behavior. She also reacts differently to seeing John in a hospital bed than she would seeing one of her former patients. Have you ever had a time when something happened to someone you loved that caused similar responses?

17. Jillian's reaction to her feelings for John was to run away—emotionally, and later in the physical sense. This caused her to feel like a fraud who could give advice but not take it. Have you ever experienced something like this?

18. There are a number of unhappy, lonely people in Jillian's new, affluent neighborhood. Comment on this.

19. Jillian's blog, "Where Broken Hearts Go," is intended to give advice for dealing with heartache in healthy ways—physically and spiritually. What advice would you give someone who was hurting, to help them deal with their heartbreak in healthy and faithful ways?

About the Author

Kathy J. Jacobson is a graduate of the University of Wisconsin-Madison and Wartburg Theological Seminary, Dubuque, Iowa. She has worked counseling troubled youth, has been an at-home Mom, a church youth worker and Christian education coordinator, worked in campus ministry, and for the last twelve years, has served in rural parish ministry. In addition to her work in the church, she volunteers as a hospice chaplain. Kathy resides with her husband in the beautiful "Driftless Area" of southwestern Wisconsin. They are parents of three children, all "twenty-something." Kathy is an avid traveler, having visited forty-nine states and five continents, with most memorable trips to Papua New Guinea, the Holy Land, and Tanzania, East Africa. She enjoys music, theater, reading, hiking, walking and hiking, but writing is her passion. This is her debut novel.

Photo by Michael Mowbray

Author's Note

Noted! is a work of fiction. It is a product of my imagination and the incredibly varied experiences with which I have been blessed, both personally and professionally. In case you are wondering, I am not "Jillian." She is much stronger than myself, and has faithfully and gracefully overcome challenges I have never personally experienced. We do share some things in common, however, such as being adopted and being raised on a small farm by two wonderful and faithful adoptive parents. We also share the same middle name, are parents of great kids, and we both love to sing. Sadly, however, I cannot play the guitar like she does. We also both left a "piece of our heart" in Tanzania. And of course, we both love to write!

Praise for NOTED!

❝We learn everything we can possibly know about Jillian and the weaknesses and negative energy that can handcuff the best of us. As Jillian struggles to find answers to some of life's toughest questions, readers begin asking the same questions of themselves.

Jillian is just one of a bevy of strong characters in Kathy Jacobson's new book that takes a refreshing look at how faith, intelligence, forgiveness and common sense can lead us through detours created by love, frustration, jealousy and uncertainty.

This is a feel-good book that everyone can identify with and enjoy!"

Rob Schultz
Reporter, *Wisconsin State Journal*, Madison, Wisconsin

❝Kathy Jacobson, writing through the adult life of Jillian, has brilliantly interwoven the dynamics of conflicted family relationships, dysfunctional courtships and marriages, and personal risk-taking!

Jillian shares her faith honestly and openly as she seeks support from God through daily prayer for herself and others.

Each of the characters' true-to-life struggles quickly bring the reader to our own reality, as we tend to join Jillian's quest for a new adventure, and for a partner who is "kind, notices things and listens to me when I speak." Could she possibly take the risk to love again?

Men and women, alike, will recognize their own struggles reflected in NOTED!"

Nancy Fulton Young
Psychologist, Marriage and Family Therapist, and Mediator
Madison, Wisconsin

❝I recently spent an evening immersed in the story of Jillian's new life. Her reflections on the past and her honest fear over how her choices today will shape the future resonated with me, and I believe they will resonate with women today; both those who have laid claim to faith and those who are yet seeking faith in God.

Kathy Jacobson brings to life the story of a woman who is imperfectly faithful to the God who loves her and who she loves in return. This is a story of the acceptance of one's own responsibility; a story of how God can bring learning, growth and grace out of any situation or decision. Jacobson's story also shows how a deeply faithful person can still have doubts and fears. Her heroine, Jillian is an "every woman" of faith; one who has made good choices and bad choices, a woman who has confidence in God's love and forgiveness but still struggles with doubt and questions.

I'd like to invite Jillian to visit the women in my community. But since that can't happen, I'd like to invite the women in my community to read "Noted" and to talk together about Jillian's life and their own. The study guide at the end of the book will be a great resource to help women consider how to reflect on their past and to step boldly into the future God has prepared for them."

Pastor Mary Lou Aune
Evangelical Lutheran Church in America